The Dreamkeepers

CHRIS BRODIEN-JONES

Bradbury Press . New York

Maxwell Macmillan Canada • Toronto
Maxwell Macmillan International
New York • Oxford • Singapore • Sydney

ACKNOWLEDGMENTS

My sincere thanks to Lisa McDuffee, who believed in *The Dreamkeepers* from the beginning; to Peter Jones, whose Welsh origins and childhood inspired the theme; and to Jo Ann Stover, whose support and literary advice helped make this book happen.

I also wish to acknowledge the Welsh towns of Blackwood and Crickhowell, upon which the imaginary town of Rhydhowell and its environs are based.

Bradbury Press
Macmillan Publishing Company
866 Third Avenue
New York, NY 10022

Maxwell Macmillan Canada, Inc.
1200 Eglinton Avenue East
Suite 200
Don Mills, Ontario M3C 3N1

Macmillan Publishing Company is part of the Maxwell Communication Group of Companies.

First edition
Printed and bound in the United States of America
10 9 8 7 6 5 4 3 2 1

The text of this book is set in 11.5 point Primer.

LIBRARY OF CONGRESS CATALOGING-IN-PUBLICATION DATA
Brodien-Jones, Chris.
The dreamkeepers / by Chris Brodien-Jones.
p.   cm.
Summary: While visiting their grandparents in a small Welsh
village, twelve-year-old Derek and his younger sister, Eve, are
caught up in a struggle between a group of ancient Dreamkeepers and
an evil sorceress.
ISBN 0-02-747862-9
[1. Supernatural—Fiction. 2. Dreams—Fiction. 3. Brothers and
sisters—Fiction. 4. Wales—Fiction.] I. Title.
PZ7.B786114Dr 1992   [Fic]—dc20   92-10884

For Ian and Derek

CONTENTS

PROLOGUE

One cold winter's night in Wales, Derek Morgan sat cross-legged on his bed, wrapped in blankets, wishing for an adventure.

The hot-water bottle under his feet had gone cold. All around him the room was dark and silent. He leaned over and looked out the window next to his bed. Penmaen Road looked very ordinary in the moonlight, and not the least bit threatening. If he squinted his eyes, he could just see the mountains that lay at the edges of Rhydhowell like humped-up dragons. But even they seemed ordinary and tame.

His nose was starting to drip. He sniffed loudly and

imagined his true identity was Tredegar Crackbone, penniless hermit inventor of sixth-century Wales. If only he could go back in time, when there were castles and priories, spells and curses and countercurses, when people had names like Boris and Gwydion.

He stared through the window, picturing Celtic settlements on the hillsides, with walls all around and Gypsies camped at the city gates. Fires burned all night long; ancient songs rang out. And of course, there would be the odd dragon or two, slinking ominously along the ramparts.

Derek shivered, pulling the covers tighter around him. He had been at his grandparents' house exactly a week, his first visit since the age of three. The plane ride from Boston to London had been a long and entertaining journey, and traveling by train to Wales had been exciting as well. Once here, he had expected intrigue, suspense, maybe some wondrous and terrible discovery that would lead to an adventure.

Instead, it had rained. It was hard to conceal his disappointment, to admit that Wales was, well, boring. Since the day he and his sister, Eve, had arrived, clothes-drenching sheets of rain had tipped down over the Welsh countryside. Grandma had made them wear rubber boots—"Wellies" she called them—and carry big black umbrellas. Even then, it was impossible to keep dry.

The rain seemed to have no effect whatsoever on Grandma. She guided them cheerfully along the muddy banks of Penyfan Pond, where Eve nearly fell in trying to feed the ducks. Soggy and disheartened, Derek had followed Grandma and Eve down dripping churchyard paths, wandering aimlessly through outdoor markets and into the damp cellars of musty, crumbling castles.

Sometimes Grandpa took them out in the car, pointing to places of historic interest. But to Derek everything looked gray and out of focus, and not very interesting at all. He wondered why his father had gone on so much about growing up in Wales, when it was so horribly wet and dreary.

Derek sniffed a few more times and looked out the window again. The sky was unusually bright. Clouds were breaking apart near the horizon, drifting away to reveal the stars beyond.

As he watched, the stars seemed to float in his direction, slowly at first, then picking up speed. He blinked a few times, as more stars appeared. It looked as if a whole galaxy was in motion, hundreds of glassy stars whirling toward Rhydhowell.

Then he realized they weren't stars at all. It was snowing! Huge, fat flakes spun downward, making him dizzy as he watched.

He sat at the window for what seemed like hours

3

but perhaps was only minutes, as snow fell in strange, hypnotic patterns. Maybe everything was going to be all right after all, he mused sleepily. Maybe the snow would bring a change. . . .

Seconds later he was asleep, while snow continued falling and dreams tumbled inside his head.

1

Snowstorm

"You have to wake up!" cried a high-pitched voice. "It's snowing, it's snowing! Wake up! Wake up!"

Derek groaned, burrowing deeper under the blankets.

"Go away, Eve," he told his sister. "It's just rain. It rains every day in Wales. Rain, rain, rain—"

"No, it's not! It's snow, and lots of it!"

Derek suddenly remembered the stars turning to snowflakes. He sprang up out of bed, throwing off the covers.

His window was glazed with a thin layer of frost,

etched with patterns of ferns and leaves. Derek scratched at the frost with a thumbnail. Through a small patch he could see the snow billowing, whirling around chimneys and off rooftops, spiraling down Penmaen Road. The entire landscape had been transformed. Houses and trees had disappeared, and the world was made up of rounded, drifting shapes.

"I can't see the mountains anymore," he said. "It's all just a white blur."

"I knew it was going to snow," said Eve smugly, "because I dreamed it three nights in a row."

"Hah," scoffed Derek. "Just dreaming something doesn't make it happen."

"Oh yes it does," she insisted. "Dreams in Wales are different, because everything here is magic. Even Grandpa says so. He told me the Black Mountains are haunted."

"Yeah, well—" Derek paused. Sometimes it didn't pay to argue with his sister.

Eve was eight years old, with spindly legs, knots in her hair, and watercolor gray eyes. She liked wearing large, out-of-date dresses, especially ones with lots of pockets, into which she stuffed bottle tops, gum wrappers, pebbles, and plastic charms. The insides of her pockets were always sticky. Grandpa called her "ragamuffin" and "my fussy urchin," particularly when she was difficult, which seemed to Derek to be most of the time. You never knew what she was going to do next.

Derek tended to go his own way, pretending Eve didn't even exist. After all, he was twelve now and had a lot of things on his mind.

School, for instance. Since September his grades had been on a downhill slide. It wasn't that the work was beyond him. He was simply bored by it. Ideas were constantly rummaging around inside his head, but his teachers didn't seem to appreciate them. "Concentrate, Derek!" Mr. Coover, his least favorite teacher, would shout halfway through math class. But trapezoids and triangles made him yawn. His mind would drift away and he would find himself sketching maps and mazes on the back of his notebook. He had serious plans of his own to be an archeologist, and needed to know practical things, like how to carbon-date fossils and positively identify the jaws of a mastodon.

"What do you call this?" his father had asked, holding up his first-quarter report card. "One B minus, three Cs, and a D. To call it mediocre would be praising it too highly, wouldn't you say?"

Derek shrugged. "Well, that D was a bit unfair. Just because old Peabrain Coover doesn't like—"

"I think I've heard enough about your Mr. Coover, Derek. Now, if we go to Wales, you have to promise you'll bring those grades back up. Nothing below a B.

I wouldn't ask if I thought you weren't capable. Understand?"

Derek nodded, secretly wishing he could beam Mr. Coover up to another planet.

Things had gone no better with his mother. "I'm trusting you to keep a sharp eye on your sister, once your father and I have gone to Scotland," she had said. His parents had made arrangements for Derek and Eve to stay in Wales, while they traveled to Glasgow to see old friends. "You know how Eve has a tendency to sometimes go astray."

He knew only too well.

Derek sighed and picked up his jeans, which lay in a heap on the floor. He pulled them on over his pajamas, a habit he'd taken up at his grandparents', because the upstairs of the house always seemed to be cold.

Eve stood drawing faces on the window with her finger. "It's always the olden days in my dreams," she said.

Where was his shirt? His sweater? Derek dropped to the floor and peered under the bed.

He could hear Eve's squeaky voice. "I dreamed about a house that looked like a castle, with a funny-looking tree outside," she was saying. "And there were people who lived inside, but I think they were really ghosts."

Derek reached under the bed and retrieved a crumpled shirt.

"Yeah, they were ghosts all right," said Eve, "because I could see right through them."

Derek stood up and looked down at a piece of Black Magic candy stuck to his knee.

"Eh, fussy urchin, what's that?" he warbled, cupping a hand to his ear. "Ghosts in your dreams?"

Eve giggled. "Stop pretending you're Grandpa."

"People in dreams aren't real," Derek told her. "That's a bunch of nonsense." He put on the crumpled shirt and began buttoning it. "It's like saying that some comic book character is going to poke his head out of the page and start talking to you."

"I'd like to meet Tweety bird," Eve said wistfully.

"What if you went to the movies and King Kong jumped out of the screen at you?"

"Yikes!" Eve's eyes were round and black. "That would be scary."

"Well, it's never going to happen. That's my point." Derek tugged at the sweater he'd gotten stuck halfway over his head. Grandma had knitted it for him, but after just a week it was all stretched out and bits of wool were unraveling. Derek felt like he was always at odds with his clothes.

Eve turned from the window and looked at him critically. "You look kind of messy," she said.

Still struggling with his sweater, Derek ignored her. Suddenly he stopped, his memory jolted. "I had a dream, too, come to think of it," he said. "I was walking underground . . . down a long, dark tunnel. Then I saw shadows moving—not shadows, really, but strange little people." He looked at Eve. "Were there any tunnels in your dream?"

"Nope," Eve answered. "Just ghosts."

After Eve had wandered from the room, Derek stood staring out the window, while bits and pieces of a dream came back to him. He still had in his mind the image of a tower, looming up from the rim of a hill. In the same dream there had been a dark tunnel, and in the distance a flickering light. As he stumbled forward, he had heard voices droning and even now could hear what sounded like "We are waiting, waiting. . . ."

Then he saw them, shadowy and twiglike, dressed in robes, carrying stacks of . . . stacks of books? He had tried to cry out but his voice was drowned by a sudden wind. Leaves spun madly around until he could no longer see the mysterious figures.

He crossed the room to the bedroom door. The dream images melted away. From downstairs came the rattle of china cups, and he could hear his grandparents and Eve moving about in the kitchen below.

"I smell bacon and eggs!" he yelled, charging down the carpeted stairs.

2

Grandpa's Adventure

A coal fire was burning in the dining room. Grandma stood beside the window, a cup of tea in her hand. She smiled as Derek bounded into the room, a boy with a solid frame, thick yellow hair, and quizzical eyes. At that age his father had looked exactly the same.

"Well now, Derek, what do you think of the snow?" she asked. "Quite a surprise really. All the forecasts were for rain."

"I can't believe it," Derek said, and grinned. "I'm going outside as soon as I can."

"You'll be wanting some breakfast first, I expect,"

said Grandma, adding, "There's tea over there, if you like."

"Thanks, Grandma." Drinking tea was a habit he had acquired since coming to Wales. He helped himself to a steaming cup, while his grandmother busied about with the breakfast things. Grandma had a cheery face and twinkling eyes—like a storybook character, Derek thought.

"Do you ever make tea in this?" Derek took an old brass teapot from the mantel and held it up. The sides were dented and the spout chipped.

"Oh, that. No, there are cracks, see, in the bottom, and the tea would leak out." Grandma shuffled over and ran her forefinger along the outside. "You can see where there was a pattern once, but it has worn away over the years."

Derek could see a faded pattern of leaves etched into the battered surface of the teapot. He wondered what sort of ancient instrument had been used to create such a design: leaves interwoven with tiny, round berries that peered from the teapot like so many eyes. "Where did it come from?" he asked.

Grandma chuckled. "Your grandpa found this just last summer, in the vegetable patch of all places. He was digging for leeks and happened on this. Our neighbor next door but one, Mr. Palethorpe, says it is ever so old."

The door opened and Grandpa trundled in, stooped and fragile as an elf. He carried a tray of plates, which rattled as he walked.

Rhys Morgan was a splintery old man who refused to tell anyone his true age. He said the best years of his life had taken place before the age of twelve, and he loved to tell conflicting versions of his past. Having married late in life, he'd hung on to his bachelor ways: frequent stops at the Owl and Unicorn Pub and solitary walks up the wooded hill behind the house, affectionately called the Tumpy.

Eve tiptoed in at Grandpa's heels, balancing glasses of orange squash on a small tray. She wore a dress Grandma had bought her at a jumble sale, with poodles ice-skating along the hem.

Breakfast was dished up, and the four ate in silence. Derek was careful not to slurp his orange squash or scrape his fork against his plate. Too many noises at the table made Grandpa wince.

When he had finished, Grandpa poured himself some tea, dark and strong, with bits of tea leaves floating on top. "Just look at the snow coming down," he said, dropping a lump of sugar into his tea and stirring it. "There'll be no getting over Cerreg Mountain by nightfall, you can be sure of that."

"Aye, Rhys," said Grandma. "We haven't seen a storm like this one for many years."

Derek turned to the window. Snow was falling thick and fast, blanketing the shed and garden wall. "Grandma, your wash is still on the line," he said, "and all the clothes look frozen."

"Oh dear," exclaimed Grandma, peering out. "I'd forgotten all about them!"

Grandpa stood up and teetered over to his armchair next to the fire. His cup rattled as he sank down into the cushions. "I remember we had a storm like this one when I was a boy." He leaned back farther in his chair, as though he were placing himself back in time. "I was just about your age, Derek, had the room upstairs that you're in now. I remember waking up, seeing the snow out my window, running downstairs and out up to the Tumpy. I was gone for hours. My dad and mam had all the neighbors out looking for me."

"Boy, they must have been mad." Eve sounded impressed.

"Worried was what they were. Found my way back, somehow, but it was awfully late. Snow was still coming down and the wind was blowing like billy-o."

"Did you get into trouble?" asked Derek.

"Not really," said Grandpa evasively. Then he continued. "Covered from head to toe with snow I was, and sort of dazed from the cold. I remember them

14

sitting me down next to the fire, wrapping me in blankets and filling me up with hot cocoa."

"They were glad to have you back, I fancy," said Grandma.

"If I did something like that," said Derek, "I'd be sent to my room."

"But where did you go, Grandpa?" asked Eve. "Did you have an adventure?"

"Well, you might say that," said Grandpa, but for once he didn't launch into one of his stories. His voice was distant and hushed. "Yes, it was certainly an adventure, and one that I've never forgotten." He put down his cup carefully, leaned back again, and closed his eyes.

"Shh," whispered Eve. "Grandpa's sleeping."

But Derek knew Grandpa wasn't sleeping at all. He was just pretending.

3

The Path to the Tumpy

Derek flew out the door and into the snow.

Thick flakes swirled around him, sticking to his hair. He ran over to the brick wall and looked at the adjoining gardens. Each plot of land, square and tidy, was filling up fast with snow.

For the past week he had felt a little homesick, thinking of his overgrown yard and tumbled bedroom, his collections of stamps and beach glass, the baseball cards scattered across his desk. At times he had yearned to be back amid the chaos of familiar things.

But now it was different. The snow had changed everything. Stumping about the back garden, he felt like an explorer, lost in time. He circled the greenhouse, its windows rimed with frost. Past the frozen washing line he trudged, over to the potting shed, built years ago by Grandpa and his father. It leaned sharply to one side, its door banging in the wind. He peered inside, disappointed to see only clay pots and a broken rake.

A stream divided the back garden from the meadow beyond, which sloped uphill to a small wood of beech trees. A path wound its way through the wood to the top of the Tumpy. When you stood up there and looked down, you could see the Morgans' house beyond the wood and the town of Rhydhowell in the distance.

"All right, then," Derek said secretly into the wind, imagining himself as young Rhys Morgan. He jammed his hands deep into his pockets and squared back his shoulders. "The Tumpy it is."

Suddenly he heard, "Hey, Derek, wait for me!" and groaned inwardly. He had seen himself marching through the drifts, a brave and solitary figure in the snow. But the image evaporated as he looked back to see Eve, racing to catch up with him. What a pest, he thought. With only her yellow raincoat and Wellington boots, she'll freeze. Eve was like a fairy-tale child, the kind who ends up being taken by trolls. And he was the one who was always having to rescue her. It wasn't fair.

"Go on back and play in the yard," he said. "I want to be on my own."

"I'm coming with you," she insisted.

"You're supposed to be helping Grandma with the mince pies."

"That's later. She's on the phone to Auntie Mair," said Eve. "Hey, don't walk so fast. These dumb boots keep coming off."

"You're not dressed for a snowstorm!" shouted Derek.

"Am too. I got loads of sweaters on under this, and long johns, too, but they're sort of itchy. And two pairs of wool socks."

"Yeah, well, okay. But I'm in charge, see, and you have to stick right by me the whole time. Understand? No running off."

Eve nodded meekly. "Righty-o," she said in a sing-song voice that annoyed Derek.

Wind gusted around them as they stamped over the frozen stream and into the meadow. The world before them was bright and unbroken, snow still falling like crystal stars. The wood was dark, a place of strangely shaped humps and shrouded trees, pierced by the eerie moaning of the wind.

Eve kept quiet, trailing Derek like a stray cat. Every

few minutes he shot a look back, making sure she hadn't wandered off. She'd done that sort of thing countless times in the past. In fact, some of Derek's earliest memories were of frantic searches for Eve through Laundromats, supermarkets, and petting zoos.

Snow had buried the path, and Derek could only guess which way to turn next. Branches clattered over their heads like bones. Their twiggy ends hooked on to his jacket collar. Eve followed, humming softly to herself.

"Wait a minute." Derek stopped and looked around, certain this was not the way to the top of the Tumpy.

"Are we lost?" asked Eve, shivering. Derek sighed and unwound his scarf, then wrapped it tightly around her neck.

"Um, well, not lost, really, no." He slipped off a mitten and reached into his pocket. "Want a bakestone?" he asked, opening up a bundle of foil. He held out the flat, currant-filled cakes.

"Yum, thanks!" Eve took two at once and stuffed one into her mouth.

"Let's keep walking," said Derek. "I'm frozen."

"We're not anywhere near the Tumpy, if that's what you think," said Eve with her mouth full. "But don't worry, I know where we are."

Derek ducked as a pine bough whipped back and forth in the wind.

"We're inside my dream," said Eve behind him.

"Oh, don't be so such a ninny. Come on, let's try this way."

As they climbed higher, things began to look more familiar. Derek felt a wave of relief. He wasn't such a bad navigator after all. Later on, he'd draw a map to this place. It was the snow that had thrown him off, but now they were all right.

They pressed on past a grove of holly bushes, which fell away as they reached a clearing. Behind him, in the distance, Derek could make out the village of Rhydhowell: the church spire, peaked roofs, the ruined castle. Clouds like tufts of wool rushed overhead, making him dizzy. I've been here before, he thought, probably with Grandpa.

Just ahead, at the rim of the hill, stood a house, dark and angular. A chill fell over Derek as he suddenly remembered.

He had never seen this house before with Grandpa.

He had seen it in a dream.

4

Ashcroft

The house towered over them, a tall, bleak shadow, its uneven roof jagged against the sky.

Eve skidded to a stop, boots sliding across the snow. Long ribbons of her hair fluttered in the wind. "That's the house, the one I dreamed about," she told him, as though she had expected it all along.

She raced on ahead and Derek followed, his heart pounding. The house was very grand, with wide stone steps running up to the main door, and what seemed to be endless rows of narrow windows, all of them shuttered. Rising up three stories, it gave the impression of having stood for centuries. Solid and dark, constructed of stone, it had an angular outline, with chimneys and gables and a steep, tiled roof.

"And the monkey puzzle tree!" Eve shouted. "That's here, too!" She ran up to an immense fir tree that grew on the sloping lawn a few yards from the house. It had long, prickly branches, which twisted strangely in all directions. Derek had never seen such a tree before.

"Grandma showed me one in a book, and she says they're magic," Eve went on, grabbing hold of one of the low, sweeping branches and hoisting herself up. "Ouch, this is sharp!"

"Grandma's always going on about magic," said Derek dryly. "She figures you're still little enough to believe all that."

"Grandma wouldn't tell lies." Eve leaned backward and fell upside down, her knees hooked over the branch. "I bet this whole place is under some creepy spell," she added darkly.

She's probably right, thought Derek, staring up at the house. At the top, framed against the sky, was a tower. The curved windows looked blank in the winter light, as if the tower was somehow in a trance. Who would want to live here? he thought. Perhaps a hermit, one who any minute would appear cursing at the window, threatening to set his dogs on them for breaking the branches of the monkey puzzle tree.

As Derek stood in the courtyard of the house, Eve swung down from the tree and skipped to the newly shoveled steps at the main door.

"Eve, where are you going now?" It was maddening, he thought, as he watched her stand on tiptoe, her hand closing around the brass door knocker. "Don't do it, Eve, they probably hate children!" The knocker fell with a dull clang.

Derek ran up the wide steps and watched as the door slowly opened. A tall, solemn-looking man with a beard stepped out, gazing down at them. He wore a patched cardigan and baggy tweeds. His copper-colored hair looked like a scribbled picture.

The gentleman cleared his throat and then spoke.

"May I help you?" he asked.

"Is it okay if I p-play in that t-tree?" stammered Eve, tilting her head back to look up at him. "The one that's magic?"

"She means the monkey puzzle tree," explained Derek.

"The monkey—? Oh, hmm, yes." The man had a deep, resonating voice and hesitated each time before speaking. "It wouldn't be a bother to me, of course, but there is Miss Harkness to consider. She might take a dim view of it."

"Miss Heartless?" Eve bent her head sideways, trying to see beyond him to the inside.

"Harkness," corrected the man. "She is the house-keeper, you see, comes in to tidy up and cook for us."

The man's eyes were green and had an opaque, weathered look, like beach glass. "I am afraid Miss Harkness runs rather a tight ship," he added.

"But does anyone else live here?" asked Eve. "Is this a haunted house?" Oh no, thought Derek, his cheeks growing red with embarrassment.

"Not haunted, exactly," said the man.

"Could we at least have a look, please?" asked Eve.

"Well, I am afraid it would be quite impossible for you to come inside now. Unfortunately it is not allowed."

Eve's lower lip began to quiver. "But I've never been in a haunted house before. It's the one from my dream."

Derek took hold of her arm. "Forget it, Eve. Let's go back to Grandma and those mince pies."

"I don't care about the mince pies!" Eve pulled away, shouting at Derek over the wind. She turned and ran down the steps, disappearing behind the house.

"Eve, come back!" Derek stood shivering as snow whirled around him in dizzying currents.

"I am sorry if I've upset your sister," said the man. "Miss Harkness is very strict and makes no exceptions."

"I'm sorry about Eve," said Derek. "She doesn't mean to be annoying."

"I understand." The man leaned against the doorway and looked down at Derek. "So where are you from, young man? Not from around here, by your accent."

"It's American," said Derek. "My sister and I flew here from Boston last week, and we're staying in Rhydhowell with our grandparents. We came up the Tumpy to do some exploring."

"I thought you looked the adventurous sort," said the man.

"I guess I'd better go look for my sister," said Derek, suddenly worried.

"Of course," said the gentleman. "But before you go, tell me, those dreams she spoke of . . . ?"

"Oh, Eve's always had dreams since she was little, dreams about goblins and elves and, oh, all sorts of things. But since coming to Wales, she's been dreaming about ghosts."

"Ghosts, you say? Of what nature?"

Derek shrugged. "They're olden-day ghosts, that's what she says, the see-through kind. And they live somewhere in this house. That's why she ran off, to find them."

The gentleman fixed his bottle green eyes on Derek.

"Welsh ghosts," Derek added impressively.

"And you? I suppose you are too old for such dreams. Consider them childish, do you?"

Derek hesitated. "No, not really," he began. "I mean, everyone dreams. I don't usually remember my dreams, but last night I dreamed I was lost in this tunnel and—" It seemed to Derek that a strange light crept into the gentleman's eyes, and he stopped speaking.

Standing there, with snow falling like confetti and the wind rushing in his ears, Derek felt balanced at the edge of the world.

"My sister is the adventurous sort, too," said Derek, in defense of Eve. "But she gets carried away with her dreams. I'm more practical."

"It saddens me to think that many of us no longer listen to our dreams," said the man. "Perhaps we should pay more attention to them."

"Do you think so?"

"Absolutely. Well, young man, perhaps it is time you retrieved your sister. I am very pleased to have met you." He held out his hand. "The name is Ashcroft."

"I'm Derek Morgan."

The two shook hands heartily, like old friends.

"If you really would like to see the inside of the house, the two of you are welcome to come back, but it would have to be after dark."

"Oh, I understand," said Derek. "Your housekeeper won't be here."

"Well, she will be here," said the man, "but if you come through the kitchen she won't see you. Through the pantry is a door, which will take you downstairs to an underground corridor. At the end of the corridor you will find my door."

Ashcroft bade him good-bye, closed the door, and disappeared inside.

"Underground corridor?" murmured Derek, suddenly remembering the tunnel in his dream.

5

Eve's Ghost

Derek ran in the direction where Eve had disappeared, to a walled-in garden adjoining the back of the house. Clumping through a stone archway, he began thinking that Grandma would worry, for they had been gone a long time. From uncurtained windows light fell across the shifting snow as it blew in glittering arcs across the garden. Black smoke poured out from a tilting chimney, gusting downward in the wind.

Derek moved slowly now, flattening himself against the wall and keeping out of sight. He came to a window, its bottom half covered with dead, snow-dusted creepers. Pushing them aside, he edged up to the sill and peered inside.

There was a thick-legged table, covered with a patterned oilcloth and piled high with crocks and mixing bowls. Scorched pots hung from low wooden rafters, and the walls, cracked in places, were a mottled gray. As he watched, a woman appeared, tall and stringy as a bean pod, carrying spoons and measuring cups. From beneath a kerchief, wisps of dry hair straggled down over the thin, pinched face.

His gaze slid over to a glass-fronted cabinet, an iron stove, and a high stool where a little girl sat nibbling a jam tart. Eve! What was she doing here? His sister chattered merrily while the woman set about her work, stirring this, pouring that, sniffing and measuring, and every so often nodding distractedly.

"As soon as I saw the monkey puzzle tree, I knew this was the house I'd dreamed about," Eve was saying. "I dreamed about the snow, too." She turned toward the window and Derek hunkered down, burying himself in the creepers. "That tall man with the beard, he said the house wasn't haunted. But I knew it had to be, because I dreamed about the ghosts."

"Don't pay any attention to Mr. Ashcroft," said the woman, frowning. "He's getting on in years and imagines things."

"Maybe he thought I meant old-fashioned ghosts,

the kind that walk around clanking chains and carry their heads under their arms."

The woman sniffed loudly as she kneaded the dough. Loose tendrils of gray hair crept out from under the kerchief. "So you have a brother, do you? The sort who gets up to no good?"

"Well, he was in trouble because he got a D on his report card." Eve helped herself to another jam tart. "Sometimes he spies on me and follows me around. That makes me really mad."

At this, Derek bristled.

"The worst sort, to be sure. You've got to outsmart this brother of yours, keep one step ahead." The woman wiped her long fingers on the apron. "Tell me now, did he dream about the ghosts as well?"

"Oh no. He had a dream about a tunnel, and some strange little people, but that's all he would tell me."

"A tunnel?" The woman's eyes narrowed to dark slits. "He dreamed of a tunnel?"

Eve shrugged. "That's what he said. But I don't think that's as interesting as ghosts, do you?" Not waiting for an answer, she slid off the stool. "I'd better be going now, Miss Harkness," she said politely. "My brother's probably looking for me right this minute."

"Just remember, keep out of his way." The old woman took out a rolling pin and flattened the lump of dough. "Don't tell him you were even here. And above all"—she smiled thinly—"don't tell him about the dreams."

"What about the ghost in the tower? Can I tell him about her?"

Miss Harkness pressed her narrow lips together. "Particularly don't mention her."

The kitchen door banged open. A man wearing a black coat and long red scarf appeared, carrying a box of groceries. He had razor-thin eyes, and his mouth was no more than a pencil stroke.

"It's all there," he said flatly, setting the box on the table.

"Mind the tartlets," snapped Miss Harkness. "What makes you so late, Zylar?"

"It's the storm, ma'am. Nearly blew me off course," he said in the same toneless voice, unwinding his scarf.

"Next time look a bit more sharp. Did you pass a boy out there?"

The man shook his head. Snowflakes melted on his oily hair. "Couldn't see my hand in front of me, the snow was that thick."

Eve slid off the stool and into her boots. "Good-bye, Miss Harkness," she said sweetly, putting on her raincoat. "I have to go back to Grandma's."

"Very well." Miss Harkness took up a bowl and furiously stirred the contents. "It's all arranged for to-night. You won't forget then, will you?"

"I'll be here."

Outside, Eve stamped over the snow toward the archway, singing to herself. Derek left his hiding place from beneath the creepers and joined her.

"Where were you all this time?" he demanded.

"It's a secret," said Eve.

"I saw you through the window," said Derek, as they trudged across the clearing. A howling wind surged around them, whipping snow against their faces. When they reached the grove of holly bushes, Derek's stomach began to rumble.

"You were talking to that horrid woman," added Derek.

"She gave me a jam tart," shouted Eve, waltzing through the snow. "A jam tart, that's all!" She whirled downhill, tripping in her big, black boots as she ran back toward the wood. Before long, her yellow shape had been swallowed up in the storm.

6

The Odd Tale of Rhonabwy Court

Derek tramped in through the back door of his grand-parents' house. The kitchen was warm and smelled of mince pies. He was exhausted and covered with snow.

Grandma poked her head through the door. "Hang up those wet things and you can join us," she said. "We're having toad-in-the-hole."

"Great!" said Derek. This was one of his favorite dishes: small, fat sausages wrapped in batter, then baked in a hot oven.

The midday meal was under way in the dining room. Derek sat down and joined the others.

"Have some beans, too, Derek," said Grandma, passing him the bowl. "We've been hearing all about the house on the hill, and the adventure you two had today."

"And the monkey puzzle tree," added Eve. "Grandma, Derek doesn't believe it's magic."

"Well, now," replied Grandma, "I expect he does, really."

Eve stuck out her tongue at Derek.

"That house is known hereabouts as Rhonabwy Court," explained Grandpa, "so named for the Welsh folk hero who dreamed of King Arthur while sleeping on a magic ox skin. It was built by monks in the early sixteenth century."

"When I was a girl, Rhonabwy Court was a home for retired coal miners. Hand over your plate, Derek." Grandma scooped up a generous portion of toad-in-the-hole. "Then it became a research center, and some librarians from the university moved in with all their books."

"Was Mr. Ashcroft in charge then?" asked Derek.

Grandpa looked up with sudden interest.

"That's right," nodded Grandma. "So you met him, did you?"

"Eve asked him if she could climb on the monkey puzzle tree, but he said the housekeeper might get mad. She's real crabby and doesn't allow visitors."

"That would be Miss Harkness. She's been at Rhonabwy for donkey's years." Grandma offered Derek a plate of buttered toast. "She's on the short-tempered side, but there you are. Someone has to keep house and cook for them. The librarians are too busy sorting through all those manuscripts."

Grandpa frowned at his plate and cleared his throat. From past experience, Derek knew that was the signal he wanted the subject changed. The meal continued in silence.

Suddenly Eve turned to Grandma. "I knew the monkey puzzle tree was magic, because it was just like the one in my dreams!"

"You're loopy," Derek told her.

"Am not. The house is real dark and spooky. Could the tree have cast a spell on it?"

"Granny Cwm always said they have the power." Grandma stood up. "I'll fetch the mince pies now."

"It's all in your head," Derek told Eve. "Magic ghosts, monkey tree spells. You've made it all up."

"I have not!" she shouted, jumping up so hard her chair fell over. "You're just jealous because your dreams don't turn real!"

"No dessert for me, thanks," said Grandpa, wincing. He walked unsteadily to his armchair by the fire, sat down, and lit his pipe.

"Try to keep your voices down, children," cautioned Grandma, returning with a tray.

She began slicing triangles of mince pie. "Rare books, religious manuscripts, hard-to-find first editions, that's what the librarians are working on," she told them. "Worth a small fortune by now, I imagine. The *South Wales Argus* ran a piece on them not long ago. It seems they have some books so old they're unable to trace the language! Our neighbor but one, Mr. Palethorpe, claims they have in their possession a book that foretells the future."

Grandpa coughed and took a few puffs on his pipe.

The storm continued for the rest of the afternoon. Derek was content to stay inside, flopped on the bed, reading *The Gorilla Hunters*. His was the smallest room in the house, and the dampest, but Derek liked it anyway, because it had been Grandpa's. He could picture Grandpa as a boy in this room reading this very same book. Looking at the old photos, he could see his grandfather as a scrappy sort of a kid, with flyaway hair and nicked knees, a knapsack flung over his back.

In the middle of chapter seven, there was a knock on his door. Grandma bustled in with a tray of hot bakestones and a mug of Ovaltine.

"Thought you could do with a bit of a warm-up. It's a bit chilly up here." She glanced around at the cluttered room, then handed Derek a postcard. "The postman's just arrived."

Derek scanned the picture on the front, then turned the card over and read it eagerly.

"It's from Mom and Dad. They're staying on the Isle of Skye, and it's snowing up there, too," said Derek. "They'll be seeing Dad's old friend in Glasgow soon."

"Oh, they must be having a smashing time." Grandma sat on the edge of the bed and reached into her pocket. "I've something else for you, Derek." She handed him a small tin box. "I found it not long ago up in the attic. It belonged to your grandfather."

Derek took the box. It was painted black and silver, with swirls of red, and there was a tiny handle on top of the lid. Derek calculated there was just enough space to fit his hamster.

"This is super! Thanks, Grandma." He gave his grandmother a hug.

"I had guessed you were something of a collector yourself," replied Grandma, smiling. She watched as Derek tried unsuccessfully to open the box. "Here, let me give you a hand. I haven't a clue where the key has gone. Rhys kept his prized possessions in here, you see. Ah, here we are. . . . "

The lid sprang open with a gentle ping.

"I'll be off now, Derek. I've left Eve downstairs with the pastry cutters."

Grandma left and Derek sat cross-legged on the bed, shaking the box upside down. Out fell three fishhooks, a sixpence, two glass marbles, a tarnished scout badge, and several needle-thin bones. Lizard bones, no doubt. Or maybe they belonged to a frog.

Derek turned the box over in his hands. It felt infinitely old. There were scratches in the paint, like faint scars.

"Hey," he said softly, "what's this?"

He lifted the lid to the box. There, wedged inside, was a paper, folded several times over, yellowed with age. Gently wiggling his finger, Derek slowly extracted it. The paper crackled as he smoothed it out on the bed.

A secret message perhaps? He tried to read it, but the words weren't even legible. The letters leaned to one side, and there were blots where the pen had leaked. It was possible that it had been written that way on purpose, in a made-up language, or some kind of code. Yet the way it was set up reminded him of verses he had copied into his notebook in Miss Arnold's English class.

Why would his grandfather keep some old poem from school?

If his father were here, he could decipher it: Translating documents was part of his job. But his father was in Scotland. Perhaps he should ask Mr. Ashcroft to take a look. Derek was certain the librarians knew a thing or two about couplets and verses and Old Welsh; they'd no doubt transcribe it in no time. As he leaned against the pillows, he could almost see their parchmentlike faces as they hunched over the crumbling pages, peering through extra-thick magnifying glasses.

He carefully folded up the poem and tucked it back into the lid.

7

In Search of Eve

While Rhydhowell slept, the wind rose and snow kept falling. The town, wrapped in white, fell into a dream. Snow piled up against walls and on rooftops, and landed on old men walking home from the pub. It glazed the windows of stalled buses and glistened on the frozen surface of Penyfan Pond. The gravestones next to Elim Church could no longer be seen. And on High Street the phone-box door was frozen shut.

The unexpected ferocity of the storm frightened some people and mystified others. They had never in their lives seen anything like it. Not in Wales, anyway.

Along Penmaen Road the streetlamps flickered and went out. The Owl and Unicorn Pub was lost in darkness. In the Morgans' house all was silent. Clocks seemed to stop ticking. No mice rustled in the attic. Derek awoke from a deep sleep and sat up in bed. It was awfully dark—darker than usual. He leaned over to the window and scraped at it with his fingernail. Snow was all he could see—great, swirling gusts of it.

The streetlights were out. Must be a power cut, he decided. He fumbled for his clothes, then dressed quickly in the darkness. By some small miracle he located his flashlight and flicked it on.

The upstairs hall was black and silent. That's funny, he thought, Eve's left her door open. Like a phantom he glided into her room.

"Eve?" he whispered, moving toward her bed.

Icy bits of snow pattered against the window. He whispered her name again.

There was no answer.

Her bed was empty.

Derek unlatched the kitchen door and walked out into the storm. Snow billowed around him, lashing at his face. The frozen wash, hanging stiff on the clothesline, glimmered in the dark. Head lowered, Derek plodded through the back garden and over the stream, wondering how much of a head start Eve had on him. This wasn't any ordinary night, he knew. Something inexplicable was taking place: a shift of some sort, a change. It had to do with the snow, the dreams, and the great stone house.

There were no signs of bootprints along the meadow. In parts, Derek found himself sinking to his knees. Eve could be anywhere; she could even be lost. His mother would be horrified, and furious—furious at him, that is. She had trusted him to make sure this sort of thing didn't happen.

As he ploughed through the deep snow, gusts of wind buffeted him backward. He concentrated on the trees and their spidery branches, the gradual slope of the land underfoot, the way the path had appeared in his dream. His legs were beginning to feel weak, rubbery, and his heart was thudding loudly against his ribs. Not much longer, he told himself.

At last the trees thinned and fell away. With relief Derek recognized the clearing and, just beyond, rising above the drifts, the towering outline of the house. Rhonabwy Court. Even its name sounded ancient and mysterious.

As he passed by, the branches of the monkey puzzle tree whispered overhead. Derek thought he could hear laughter floating down from the tower, but soon it faded away.

At the back of Rhonabwy Court, inside the walled garden, pale light spilled from the windows. The rest of the house lay in darkness. Derek knocked on the kitchen door, but no one answered. He pushed the door open and stumbled inside.

The kitchen was filled with long shadows and there was a smell of boiled cabbage. He wrinkled his nose and shivered, thinking longingly of Grandma's steamy kitchen, of chips sputtering in oil, and the smell of freshly brewed tea. Leaving the chilly kitchen behind, he strode boldly into the next room, looking for Eve. An unexpected sight awaited him.

On every wall there were shelves from floor to ceiling. Rows and rows of shelves, carved of polished wood, all of them empty.

The next room was the same, with only shelves and not a stick of furniture. And the librarians, where were they? Why weren't they settled into easy chairs, reading dusty old books with crumbly pages? Why weren't they sitting at card tables, playing chess or Lexicon word games? A shutter banged against the house and he jumped, startled. Gazing through a window into the darkness, he suddenly realized how late it really was—past midnight. The librarians would have gone to bed hours ago.

"Eve!" he called, running to the next room and beginning to panic. All he could hear was the low moaning of the wind, rattling the windows of Rhonabwy Court.

Out of breath, Derek reached the front hallway and the main staircase. A warning voice sounded in his head, telling him not to go up.

But he gripped the banister and took a step. He climbed slowly, a knot tightening in his stomach.

Pausing on the second-floor landing, he waved his flashlight down a hall with doors on both sides, all of them closed. The stairs continued up, opening onto the third floor, where he found himself staring down another hallway. Here he counted three doors in all: a paneled door, halfway down on the right, and across from this, an odd little door with mullioned windows, opening onto a balcony. The third door stood ajar at the far end of the hall. When he looked at this last door, the hairs on his scalp prickled faintly.

He approached the far door warily, cobwebs fluttering overhead.

As he reached for the handle, he heard Eve laughing.

8

Iona

The door opened onto a short flight of steps, which curved up to a room all on its own. The tower! thought Derek, remembering the first time he had seen it, as he stood under the monkey puzzle tree.

He stepped into a five-sided room, with a pitched roof and windows all around. As in his grandmother's attic, thick, sturdy beams ran overhead. An iron hoop with candles along the rim hung from the apex of the tower. Wax dripped down to the polished floor below, and a smell of smoke hung in the air.

Through the windows he could see the sky. The

snowstorm had subsided and stars shone brilliantly. The wind was singing through the icicles, which hung in jagged points outside the high, arched windows. The stars and ice and candle flames blurred into one mysterious light.

He tiptoed forward. Next to the far window a woman was seated on a spindle-backed chair, leaning toward Eve, who sat listening at her feet. He moved closer to hear what they were saying.

"I spent my childhood in the Ice Forest," said the woman. "It is a splendid place, where the shadows are long and where icicles tinkle from the branches of trees. The sky is a dark, dark blue, like an overturned bowl, with dazzling stars of crystal. . . ."

"I wish I could go there," said Eve in an awestruck voice. "I wish I could go there this very minute!"

"Perhaps one day we shall. Oh, and there are strange, wondrous animals that swim in the cold green waters. They dwell on slabs of ice, just below the surface. Like seals they are, but much furrier, with great black eyes and wet noses."

Eve was silent.

The woman continued in a cold and brittle voice. "You are apt to find, along the riverbanks, snow caves and fairy snow castles that overhang the river's edge."

"Fairy snow castles?" Eve was breathless with excitement. "Oh, please take me there, please, please!"

Derek could see the woman's long fingers lacing and interlacing. She wore rings of silver with enormous stones that seemed filled with a strange, cold light. Had he dreamed about her before? She seemed so familiar. He had heard her voice somewhere, and even the way she moved reminded him of someone. . . . Distractedly he stopped to watch a star shoot across the sky, framed in the window before him.

A freezing voice cut through his reverie. "What on earth are you doing here?" demanded the woman, rising to her feet, glowering at him.

"I just c-came to get m-my sister," said Derek, taking a step backward.

Eve looked up from the floor, where she sat hugging her knees, but she gave no sign of recognition.

The woman was tall, like a tree in winter, with a sharp, knowing face and glittering eyes. Her silver hair was twisted in a knot on top of her head. Over her bony frame was thrown a dress that looked like a spangled curtain. Derek knew at once she was timeless and ancient, in spite of her unwrinkled face and slender, unblemished hands.

"She has to come home now," he went on bravely. "Grandma will worry because it's so late."

"Late?" repeated the woman contemptuously. "There is no such thing here as late or early. There is no such thing as time." She fixed her silver eyes on him, enormous eyes that seemed to be made of a thousand tiny mirrors.

Eve stood up, gazing around at the room. "I want to go there right now," she said wistfully. "I want to go where the fairy snow castles are. . . ."

"But we shall, we shall, my dear," said the woman sweetly. She turned back to Derek. "You should never have come here." Her voice was suddenly low and threatening.

I know that voice, he thought. I've heard it before. Then he realized what he had known all along.

"I know who you are," he said defiantly. "You're the housekeeper, Miss Harkness."

"Yes, it is true," she said, moving light as a spider toward him. "The villagers of Rhydhowell all know me by that name. But that's just a little game we play, Mr. Ashcroft and myself. . . ." Her pale lips curved into a thin, unpleasant smile.

"Eve, let's go!" Derek shouted, running over to his sister and shaking her by the arm.

"I don't want to," Eve said stonily. "I want to stay here with my new friend, Iona."

"Eve, she's the housekeeper, Miss Harkness."

"Her real name, her true name, is Iona. And her real home is an ice forest. She's going to take me there to see the fairy castles made of snow. And the black, furry animals like seals."

"Don't be silly, Eve—"

But she was off, flitting away toward Iona Harkness. The two clasped hands and glided out the door.

"Wait!" cried Derek, running after them down the curved steps. Miss Harkness and Eve were at the far end of the hall. He watched as they disappeared down the main staircase.

As he stood there, undecided, two skeletal hands gripped him by the shoulders.

"Spying, is it?" snarled a man with black eyes and oily hair. It was the man who had delivered groceries to Miss Harkness, the one she had called Zylar.

"Hey, let go!" Derek wriggled and tried to pull away.

"Iona Harkness does not allow spies in the house," said Zylar in a raspy voice. Hooking one hand onto Derek's collar, he marched him down the hallway, stopping halfway, at the paneled door.

"I'll teach you to spy, I will. You'll think twice next time." Zylar brushed away the strands of cobwebs and kicked the door with a pointed boot.

"Go on, then," he ordered, and they clattered down a narrow, unlit stairway, wooden boards creaking underfoot. Derek counted one, then two floors, and finally a third, which he guessed was the cellar. Zylar elbowed the door open and pushed Derek into a damp passageway, which smelled of roots and rotted earth.

"Where is this?" shouted Derek as a cold wind struck his face. "Are we outside?"

"We are not." Zylar's laugh was a dry rattle in his throat.

"Let go of me!" cried Derek, pulling away. "Let go, you slimy toad!"

Zylar's fingers dug deeper into his arms.

Derek reached out blindly, running his hand along the passage wall. The earth felt frozen beneath his fingers. He had no idea in which direction they were going, and each step left him more uncertain. The cellar seemed to be a honeycomb of twisting tunnels. Where was the kitchen, the walled-in garden, the monkey puzzle tree?

His boot caught on a root, or maybe it was a pile of old bones. He stumbled and, for an instant, the bony fingers let go. Sensing freedom, Derek whirled around, pushing his captor aside, and raced back in the direction they had come.

"Come back!" screamed Zylar. "Come back, you young fool! You'll never find your way out!"

Derek ran on, a freezing wind at his back, Zylar's footsteps echoing close behind. He chose tunnels at random, racing up one and down another, as new fears sprang up in his mind. What if the walls collapsed around him, trapping him inside? What if there was someone—or something—waiting up ahead?

By now the thud of Zylar's boots had died away. After what seemed like hours, Derek saw the outline of a door. Reaching out, exhausted, he called out, stumbled, and fell. Blackness enveloped him.

9

The Plague of Dark Dreams

When he awoke Derek found himself on a sofa, with blankets tucked all around, in a tiny room with no windows. There were stacks of books on the floor and half-empty cups of tea lying about. The room was lit by candles melting into saucers. In one corner stood a rolltop desk littered with feather pens, ink bottles, and scrolls of parchment.

"Where am I?" he blurted out.

"It seems you lost your way out there," came a familiar voice. Mr. Ashcroft took a kettle from a hook over a coal fire and poured steaming water into a teapot.

"Have a cup of tea, now, you're looking a bit peaky."

"Peaky's not the word." Derek sank back into the cushions. "I was almost thrown in with the skeletons."

"The . . . ? I don't quite catch your meaning." Mr. Ashcroft handed him a cup of tea. Bits of curdled milk floated on top. Closing his eyes, Derek sipped it.

"That's better." Mr. Ashcroft regarded him with his dark green eyes. "Had a bit of a turn, have you?"

"I was following Eve and Miss Harkness out of the tower when Zylar grabbed me," said Derek. "He took me down to the cellar into a freezing cold tunnel. And he wouldn't let go of me."

Ashcroft raised his thatched brows. "Sounds most unpleasant. The tower, you say? What were you doing up there? I explained quite clearly you were to come here. Rhonabwy Court can be most unpredictable at night."

"I realize that now," said Derek. "But what could I do? Eve sneaked out of the house in the middle of the night, and I had to find her."

"Iona has a talent for charming people, and at night her powers become stronger," Ashcroft said grimly. "It would be simple for her to mesmerize your sister."

"She's a hypnotist?" asked Derek, and set down his cup. "I'm really confused. Everybody in this place seems to talk in riddles. I thought she tidied up for the librarians. Isn't that what you are? A librarian?"

"Well . . . let's just say I was at one time a librarian," said Ashcroft, pouring them each another cup of tea.

Derek frowned. "What are you then?" he asked, his gaze falling on a tattered cloak, which hung beside the fire. It was dark green velvet, with a border of gold leaves. "Are you some sort of wizard? Or conjurer?" His father had always warned him to be on the lookout for conjurers.

"Hmm, not exactly," replied Ashcroft with a bemused smile. "We are, I daresay, a cut above that."

Ashcroft crossed the room and settled his gaunt frame into a wooden bench. Carved into the back was what seemed to be a pattern of interlacing leaves.

"So where are the librarians?" asked Derek. "And the library? What happened to all the books?"

"There was a time when this house overflowed with books—amazing, light-filled volumes written by the Dreamkeepers," explained Ashcroft. "Scholars, priests, and pilgrims journeyed here from all ends of the earth. We were a center of great wisdom and healing. Small, winged creatures called the Llanellith were entrusted with the pages from these books." He paused, running his fingertips over the carvings on the bench. "You can see them here, chiseled into the wood. Each night, they left the tower, carrying Dreams to the villagers. After a time Rhydhowell evolved into a place of kindness and well-being.

It acquired, so to speak, a kind of grace."

"Rhydhowell?" Derek was skeptical. "But that's an awful place! I've been to High Street lots of times with Grandma, and everyone is sort of grouchy, and rude. People are always grumbling to one another, and their houses and gardens are all run-down. They don't seem to care about anything. Grandma says they're bitter because they've lost hope, but I don't know why they should feel that way."

"Ah, but they have lost hope," said Ashcroft gravely. "You see, one Dreamkeeper, many years ago, became greedy. He wanted the power of the Dreams. With a map torn from an old book, he set off for the Ice Forest, far to the north. When he returned, we no longer recognized him. He was accompanied by a woman from that dark, cold region, and she had by then made him her servant. . . ."

"Zylar!" exclaimed Derek.

Ashcroft nodded. "He has paid many times over for his treachery, you may be sure. And, sadly, Zylar has forgotten the ways of the Dreamkeepers. His heart is now cold and knotted."

"No wonder he's such a toad," said Derek.

"Once she had won over Zylar, Iona moved quickly, gaining entry to Rhonabwy Court. She first took over the libraries, taking one floor at a time, then the tower. When she took the tower, only a few of us escaped.

During the night, when her power is at its peak, we come down here, to the tunnels. We have ways of preventing her dark dreams from reaching the town. But now she is becoming stronger, while our power is diminishing."

"So the dreams Eve had were from Iona?"

"Exactly." Ashcroft stood up. "To be sure, many of her dreams at first appear most lovely—and therein the danger lies, for underneath they are filled with selfishness and despair."

"But my dreams were different from Eve's," said Derek. "Though we both dreamed about the path up the Tumpy. . . ."

"The Dreamkeepers sent you those Dreams, hoping they would lead you here. We desperately need your help, you see." Ashcroft snatched his cloak from the peg. "It may already be too late."

"Too late for what?" asked Derek, catching the smaller cape Ashcroft tossed him.

"Wrap that around you," ordered Ashcroft. "The tunnels are cold."

In his green velvet cloak and sandals, Ashcroft seemed mysteriously changed. He was taller somehow, seemingly alone in a magic world, his copper beard flashing in the light of the fire.

"I shall take you now," he said, "to the Hall of the Dreamkeepers."

10

In the Hall of the Dreamkeepers

Derek followed Ashcroft down the earthen channel, running to keep up with his long-legged stride. He could smell leaves and upturned soil, and an old vegetable smell that reminded him of Aunt Ethel's root cellar in Wisconsin. This must be what it was like to be a mole, he decided, not liking it much.

An archway of woven roots led into a long, raftered hall. The room was filled with a warm yellow light and the smell of woodsmoke. A fire blazed within a crumbling stone hearth. Candles burned in glass holders placed on tables amid notebooks, pens, and pairs of spectacles.

The earthen walls were shored up with slabs of granite; leaning against them were row upon row of leather-bound books, towering up on all sides. Crammed higgledy-piggledy into the shelves were battered old volumes with marbled edges, similar to those Derek had seen in Ashcroft's room.

At the center of the hall was a table of rough-hewn wood. On long benches placed on either side were the Dreamkeepers, scribbling furiously across the pages of books. They looked just the way Derek rememberd from his dreams, thin and frail, like bundles of twigs beneath their long robes, with nut-brown skin and hair like dried moss. Derek watched as they dipped quill pens into pots of gold ink, their movements swift and light.

"As you can see," said Ashcroft, "there are precious few of us left." Derek counted eight. What had happened to the others?

One Dreamkeeper set down his pen and looked up mournfully at Derek. His white beard trailed over the pages, and his eyes were emerald green.

"Are these people, um, related to you?" Derek asked Ashcroft.

"Hmm, an interesting question. You might say we share the same origins," replied Ashcroft, "and our lives span many more years than ordinary people's. Dreamkeepers are old souls, you see; they live for centuries. I am known as Lord of the Dream-keepers."

"Lord of the Dreamkeepers," repeated Derek.

"Now, if you don't mind, I shall introduce you," said Ashcroft, his deep voice resonating throughout the hall. "This is young Derek Morgan. Our Dreams have reached him more swiftly than we had expected, and he has come this night to offer his help."

There was a murmur of excited voices and a nodding of heads. Derek's smile faded. What had Ashcroft meant by that? He stared back at eight pairs of dark green eyes. Were they expecting him to say some-thing? He lowered his head, feeling suddenly shy.

"Morgan, is it?" said a Dreamkeeper at last. "The very image of Rhys."

"Not so slight, as I recall," added another, "but lively enough."

"Sturdy-looking chap," piped up another. "I'll back him!"

Derek looked up at Ashcroft with a quizzical expres-sion. Ashcroft was smiling. "Welcome to the Hall of the Dreamkeepers," he said. "We have waited for you a long time."

"A long time indeed," echoed one of the twiglike people. "Two generations to be exact!"

The Dreamkeepers laughed, a sound like rustling leaves.

In the Hall of the Dreamkeepers, Derek sat beside the fire in an armchair, reading a book about pirates. The pages were spotted, and some crumbled as he turned them.

"What's that, Mr. Ashcroft?" he asked suddenly. "That funny-looking white bug?" He pointed to a chalky white beetle with pincers scuttling across the hearth. It was the size of a half-dollar and looked like a trilobite.

Quills dropped. Heads shot up.

"Kill it at once!" shouted a Dreamkeeper, rushing over. He stamped down on it with a sandaled foot.

All that was left was a pile of dust.

"I had a fossil once that looked like that," Derek said, staring down at it. "What is it, anyway?"

"Usk Beetle," murmured the Dreamkeeper, turning away.

"Never heard of them," said Derek. "It sounds Egyptian."

"Not at all. They come from Wales." Ashcroft said, offering yet another cup of tea. "Iona sends them here often, the Usk Beetles. They have acquired a taste for parchment and ink, and their attacks are swift and unpredictable. We have lost hundreds of books."

"Wherever did Iona Harkness find them?"

"Creatures such as she have a talent for making dead things come to life," said Ashcroft. "She dredged them up from the River Usk, which lies to the east of Rhydhowell. They date back before the dinosaurs."

"Then they really are fossils!" said Derek, astonished. "Do you think I could take one home with me, to show Ms. O'Fyfe, my science teacher?" Secretly he thought it might improve his grades.

The Dreamkeepers gazed at him in stony silence.

"Maybe not, then." Derek gave a small sigh. He could imagine presenting one to his science-minded father. He'd certainly be impressed.

"Such things are not of your world and are best left here," came Ashcroft's reply. "To meddle with the Usk Beetles could well prove disastrous."

Nodding solemnly, the Dreamkeepers murmured in agreement. Derek stared at the hearth again. The pile of chalklike dust was gone, as if the Usk Beetle had never existed.

11

Trapped in the Spell of Ice

For Derek the rest of that night was like one of his dreams.

The Dreamkeepers were indeed old souls, with somber eyes and a formal way of speaking. Like kindly aunts and uncles, they offered him bits of chocolate and licorice twizzles, and asked him about school. They wanted to know which books were his favorites, nodding with approval when he mentioned books like *The Three Musketeers*, *The Coral Island*, and *King Arthur and the Knights of the Round Table*.

He peered over their shoulders as they wrote in the Dream books. Their writing looked like splinters of light wheeling across the parchment.

"How do your Dreams reach people?" he asked a Dreamkeeper.

"A simple matter, really," she replied, throwing Derek a wrinkled smile. Pointing to a glass orb on the table, she told him to look closely.

He saw within the orb a flutter of delicate wings. There were three of them, mysterious creatures shot through with light, no larger than one of Grandma's thimbles.

"The Llanellith," she explained. "Ancient deliverers of the Dreams."

"They're beautiful," said Derek.

"The Dreams enter their wings, you see, and they fly into the town to deliver them. We have now only three, and a shame it is, when once there were scores of them."

"The other Llanellith vanished when Iona Harkness appeared," added another. "No one knows where they've gone."

The orb was lifted, and the mysterious Llanellith flew out. They were transparent, sticklike creatures, reminding Derek of dragonflies. Floating silently up to the rafters, they paused, then glided down, hovering above the open books. As the Llanellith skimmed across the pages, their wings seemed to absorb the golden hue of the ink.

"They once flew each night from the tower," said the Dreamkeeper. "But since Iona took the tower from us, they have grown terribly weak." She indicated a narrow opening between two bookshelves that funneled skyward. "Now when they carry the Dreams, they must travel up that space just there. It is some sort of ancient chimney, you see, and leads to the outside."

Derek twisted his head and peered up the chimney. Wet snowflakes spiraled down, landing on his forehead and lashes.

"We are fearful, however," the Dreamkeeper continued in a quavering voice, "that they will not survive much longer without the tower. . . ."

"Come, Derek," said Ashcroft, and they set off down a cold, windswept tunnel, heading deep within the unlit maze of corridors. Before long, Derek had lost all sense of direction, and his legs were aching.

"I can't go much farther, Mr. Ashcroft," he murmured groggily. "Really I can't."

They negotiated a few more turns, and at last Ashcroft slowed down as they reached an archway in the rock. "Look through and tell me what you see," he said.

Derek swiped at his nose with his sleeve. He gazed through the rough opening. He saw a room with curved walls and a high, vaulted ceiling. There were no windows, yet snow seemed to be falling. As his eyes adjusted to the wintry light, he saw a line of frozen figures. They reminded him of winter images from childhood, the ones he used to shake inside crystal globes. Only the snow was moving, while the figures remained perfectly still.

"Those are Dreamkeepers!" he gasped, staring with disbelief at the forms locked inside glistening layers of ice. Stacks of books towered up behind them. They seemed fixed in a trance of eternal winter.

"But . . . they're still alive, aren't they, Mr. Ashcroft?" whispered Derek.

"Perhaps they are. We are not certain, of course," he replied. "These were the Dreamkeepers caught by surprise, trapped in Iona's spell of ice. We've not been able to free them these long years."

"How could she?" Derek cried. "It's not fair! We have to get them out of there!"

Ashcroft shook his head wearily. "It is no use, Derek, we've tried."

"Maybe a blowtorch! Or we could use dynamite: Blast them out of there! There must be some way."

"Have you seen enough, then, Derek? I am afraid it is getting late, and both of us are weary." They trudged back down the tunnel, ice clinging to their hair and cloaks, toward Ashcroft's chamber.

Derek desperately wanted to help the frozen Dream-keepers escape, but he didn't know how. How could anyone undo such a terrible spell? He stumbled, dazed, back into Ashcroft's room and collapsed on a heap of cushions, instantly falling asleep.

And dreamed. Dreams of a silver-eyed sorceress floating across the tiled roof of the house. Usk Beetles swimming through the air like snowflakes. A river sweeping past the monkey puzzle tree. And there was Eve, balanced on an ice floe. "Follow me, Derek!" she called. "The fairy snow castles are over here!"

The ice floe was breaking apart, and he tried to warn her, but no sound came. Helplessly, he watched as the ice disintegrated. There was a splash. When he looked again, Eve was being swept down the river, toward a forest of ice.

He awoke suddenly to a burning smell. He could see Ashcroft kneeling beside the fire, scraping a piece of toast with a knife.

"Not one of my better efforts," he chuckled, carrying over a tray of tea and the scraped toast. "Just find your way around the burnt bits."

"Thanks," said Derek, chewing hungrily. "I have to be getting back after this." He thought a moment. "I hope Eve can find her way down the Tumpy," he added.

"No doubt she will."

"Miss Harkness couldn't, well, *keep* Eve, could she?" Derek asked, wondering if Eve would go off to the Ice Forest with Iona Harkness.

"It is not quite that simple." Ashcroft's face had a hard, stony look. His hair stood up like tufts of burnt grass. "The dreams Iona sends to her have a swift and fearful power. They will continue to draw your sister back to Rhonabwy Court.

"Iona is aging, you see. In time she will crumble away, like the Usk Beetle you saw crushed tonight. If she dies, the dark dreams will die also. And so she is looking for a successor, someone to carry on her work, someone to send out the dark dreams."

Derek sat dumbfounded, letting Ashcroft's words sink in. "You mean, she wants Eve to take her place?"

"I believe so," said Ashcroft, his voice grim. "Once Eve has joined Iona, the dark dreams will continue."

Derek retrieved his jacket and mittens, which had been left to dry beside the fire. "Is there anything we can do?" he asked.

"Indeed there is," said Ashcroft, opening the door for him, "now that you have come."

With a puzzled frown, Derek stepped out, and the door closed behind him.

12

At the Red Dragon Café

Bundled in warm clothes, Derek and Eve tagged behind Grandma on her shopping rounds. Snow fell lightly along High Street as they went in and out of the shops. By late morning their arms overflowed with packages of currant buns and pork chops, tobacco and washing-up liquid, horehound lozenges for Grandpa's tickly throat.

Derek stumped over the hard-packed snow, thinking of the terrible silence of Rhydhowell. The streets were ghostly and quiet. The wind blew powdery drifts against the shopfronts, and occasionally an icicle cracked as it broke off an awning.

The townspeople milled about aimlessly, eyes darting and suspicious, or else wrapped in secret thoughts, like sleepwalkers. The parks and buildings had a neglected air, and everything looked worn and crumbly. Shopkeepers and customers argued; mothers forgot to comfort their babies. No children played in the streets, shouting and laughing. A deep lethargy had settled over the town.

"Last stop, then." Grandma paused outside the newsagents'. "Perhaps you'll find one of those comics you like so much, Eve."

Eve made a beeline to the comic books as soon as they were inside. *Dandy* and *Beano* were her favorites. Derek noticed the comics were old and tattered, like everything else in the shop. He peered inside a row of dusty jars. The sweets inside looked like they'd been there forever.

He went back to Eve, who was absorbed in a comic, moving her lips with the words.

"Eve," he whispered in her ear. "Where did you go when you left the tower? Tell me."

She twitched her shoulder and moved away. "There's nothing to tell," she said, and kept on reading.

Angrily, Derek snatched the book away.

"You don't scare me one bit," said Eve, pulling a

hideous face at him. "She said you'd try to trick me into not going back. Well, I'll do what I want. That old man with the beard made everything up. That's not his house, and he isn't a librarian."

"Miss Harkness isn't really the housekeeper, either."

"Of course she isn't," Eve sneered. "She captured the house from those dream-creatures, and now it belongs to her. She can do anything she likes!"

"It's not her house."

"It is too," insisted Eve. "And she told me all about how she makes up dreams. 'Winter-dreams,' she calls them. And she's promised to take me to the Ice Forest to see the fairy snow castles. But you can't come. She doesn't like you."

"I don't like *her*."

Eve narrowed her eyes at him. "You'd better watch out, Derek Morgan, or she'll turn you into a frog."

"She'd better not try," bristled Derek. "And you just keep away from her. Do you understand?"

"You can't tell me what to do!" cried Eve, kicking him in the shin.

Derek lunged at her, pulling her hair, and they tumbled over. The magazine rack fell with a crash, scattering comic books over the floor.

"Children!" cried Grandma. "Whatever is going on?"

"They're all that way nowadays," muttered the newsagent, raking his hands through his hair. "Chil-

70

dren 'round here, all they do is fight. Hooligans, all of 'em."

"Grandma, was Rhydhowell always so gloomy?" asked Derek.

The three of them sat in the Red Dragon Café, drinking cocoa and eating buttered scones. Derek and Eve had won Grandma over by tidying the comic rack and buying a copy of *Beano*, then apologizing to the newsagent.

Eve piled her scone high with jam. "The people in this town are sort of like ghosts," she said, "except you can't see through them. It's like the fairy tales where some old castle and all the people in it are under a spell." She bit into the scone, dripping jam on the tablecloth. "Then again, maybe they're aliens. Maybe they flew here from outer space."

Grandma shook her head. "It wasn't always this way," she said, looking intently at the children with her bright blue eyes. "When your grandpa and I were children, Rhydhowell was a grand place to be. Everyone was so friendly and cheerful, and there was music and singing. In those days, I remember, people seemed to enjoy themselves more often than they do now."

"So what happened?" asked Derek.

"I really couldn't say," Grandma replied. "It was slow in coming on, like, but over the years people began to close in on themselves. They grew inward and quiet, as if they'd forgotten how to be happy. Of course, Granny Cwm saw it differently. She said the town had fallen under a curse. In her later years she used to talk about the dark dreams."

Derek stiffened. His hand was shaking as he reached for his cup of cocoa.

Eve didn't seem to notice. "Sounds kind of scary," she said.

"Granny Cwm was getting on, naturally, perhaps a bit confused in her later years. Still, I wonder sometimes—"

"But Grandma, why didn't you move away?" asked Derek. "Why did you stay in Rhydhowell when it was so awful?"

"Because your grandfather wouldn't hear of moving, that's why. 'Let's buy a house over Abergavenny way,' I'd say, 'or what about Fishguard, on the coast?' But no, he wouldn't budge, not your grandpa." She stirred her cocoa thoughtfully. "I don't know what's held him so fast to Rhydhowell all these years, but something has. It is a mystery to me, but there you are. I suppose I'll never know."

Snow was coming down thick and fast as they left the Red Dragon Café. In the dusky light they made their way to the top end of High Street to catch the return bus home.

A small group of shoppers huddled in the shelter, grumbling about the bus being late. A short woman in a furry hat described how she had been pushed aside in the bus queue the previous day. "Cheeky little thing, he was," she said. "Jabbed his elbow into my side, he did." The old ladies clicked their tongues, eyeing Derek as if it were his fault. He shrank back against the shelter wall.

Fifteen minutes later the bus lumbered up to the stop. It was a double-decker. Eve became instantly excited and demanded that they ride on top.

"Grandma's too tired, Eve," said Derek.

"It's all right," said Grandma. "We'll go have a look up top."

Derek followed them up an iron stair. The bus smelled the way that only British buses could smell: a mixture of upholstery and cigarettes and damp wool. Eve sat in the front row, peering out the large, smut-stained window. The bus shuddered and lurched ahead, noisily shifting gears.

"Grandma?" said Derek. "What was it Granny Cwm said about the dark dreams? Did she really believe in them?"

"Oh yes, she certainly did." Grandma rummaged

through her enormous pocketbook. "She said that over the years there had been strange dreams in Rhydhowell. Unsettling, she called them. Dreams that took away people's goodness and their capacity for joy." She snapped her purse shut, handing Derek and Eve each a coin. "Here, give this to the conductor when he passes."

The bus crunched to a halt in the snow and more passengers boarded. Eve bounced up and down on the seat. "Mind those sticky fingers," cautioned Grandma. A man with a beaklike face collected their fares. Derek leaned back and closed his eyes. He felt sleepy, lulled by the warmth inside the bus.

The engine rumbled again, and the bus crept forward.

"Well, hello," he heard Grandma say, "fancy seeing you here. I have my grandchildren with me today. They've come all the way from America. Eve and Derek, say hello to Miss Harkness."

Derek's eyes flew open.

He spun around, finding himself face-to-face with Iona Harkness. Under the harsh lights of the bus she looked old and rickety, dwarfed inside a woolen coat. Her face looked penciled-in, there were so many wrinkles, and the gray hair was scraped back beneath a drab scarf. Her long, gloved fingers were clasped around a package in her lap.

74

"Hello, children," she said mildly.

"Hello, Miss Harkness," sang Eve, bobbing up in her seat. "Grandma's bought us Chelsea buns and jam tarts."

"How lovely," replied the old woman. "Aren't you lucky to have such a kind grandma."

Derek gazed at Iona in silent astonishment. Had she followed them into Rhydhowell?

The centers of her eyes were like pinpoints of ice. They held him, drawing him across a flat, snowy plain, pulling him into a dark, cold place. A chill fell over him. He shivered, forcing himself to look away.

"And how are things at Rhonabwy Court?" asked Grandma. "One hears so many rumors."

"Oh, quiet. Very quiet," said Miss Harkness. "Quiet as a tomb."

Derek shuddered.

"Is it now? A pity really." Grandma shifted the parcels in her lap. "The library used to positively hum with activity, didn't it? And the books! You couldn't see from one end to the other for all the books."

"Most of the books are gone now, I'm afraid, and only a handful of librarians are left." Iona's voice was sharp, like an icicle cracking in the wind. "And old Mr. Ashcroft, he's not at all well. Been in poor health for some time now. His eyesight is failing, and his memory isn't what it was. I'm afraid he's begun imagining things lately."

"Oh, dear, I am sorry," clucked Grandma. "He was such a brilliant chap. Knew ever so much about literature."

Against his will, Derek turned and looked back at Iona. There was a cold, remorseless light in her gaze. Derek felt as if he were sinking. Wind sang in his ears. The bright lights dimmed and voices seemed to float around him, fading in and out. He could no longer see the real world at all.

His body ached all over. He felt bone-weary.

He saw Rhydhowell, not as it appeared out the window, but at some future time. The town lay in ruins. Snow billowed down the empty streets. Centuries went by, burying the crooked peaks and steeples and rooftops. When at last the archeologists discovered it, using picks to break through the layers of snow, they would find only—

Only what? *Bones and ice*, laughed the voice— Iona's voice—*Bones and ice.*

The interior of the bus swam into view, and Derek wrenched his gaze from Miss Harkness, turning round to face the window. His teeth were chattering, and the tips of his toes and fingers felt numb.

Snow brushed against the windows of the bus. Too much snow! How could he possibly make it through those drifts? They were so high, and cold, freezing cold.

Iona was too clever. It was a losing battle, and he was tired. He'd never find his way back now. *Be quiet now*, the voice told him. *There is nothing you can do. Lie down in the snow and rest.*

"Derek? Derek?" Grandma's worried face floated before him. "Are you all right?" she asked.

Snow drifted in circles around him, shimmering patterns that lulled him to sleep. . . .

13

Eve's Dream

Surrounded with pillows, Derek sat in bed, an afghan around his shoulders and a steaming bowl of herbs in his lap. Every two minutes he threw a towel over his head and breathed deeply, as Grandma had instructed.

Eve clumped around the room in high heels and a starchy gown that Grandma had worn over thirty years before to Cousin Gwennie's wedding. "Zylar, see to those Usk Beetles," she commanded. "We are going now to the Ice Forest, so pack your mittens and long johns! It is a long journey, my dears."

Derek peered from under the towel. "Eve?" he rasped, then began to cough again.

She paid him no attention. He slumped back into the pillows. All night long he had been delirious with a raging fever. He had dreamed about trilobites and the Red Dragon Café and bus rides over landscapes of ice and snow. Halfway through the night he'd woken up in a cold sweat.

"We are here at last, in the Ice Forest. Oh, look my dears! There's a fairy snow castle." Eve made her voice go deep: "Miss Harkness, what are those teeny footprints?"

Eve brandished a wand Grandma had made from a dowel and a cardboard star. Her eyes looked frosted over, like the windows. "Why, Zylar, don't you know, those belong to the teeny tiny fairies. Look, there's one now!" She leaped on the bed and stirred the air with her wand.

"Hey, watch out, you'll spill the herbs," warned Derek.

Eve jumped up again and crashed to the floor.

"You're off your head," muttered Derek, retreating back under the towel.

The door opened and Grandma appeared, carrying a tray of tea and cakes. "Eve, do get off the floor. Mind, don't trip on your hem."

She set down the tray beside Derek. "Just what the

doctor ordered, don't you think?" She smiled at him.

Eve sat up and looked over the edge of the bed. "The fairies will like these," she said.

"Settle down now, Eve," Grandma said in a stern voice. "I can tell you're getting overexcited."

Eve sat obediently on the bed, frowning. Grandma poured the tea and handed them each a cup. "I'll leave you to it, then," she said, and bustled out of the room.

"I don't like tea," Eve pouted. "It makes my teeth feel funny."

"It doesn't do that to me," said Derek. "Grandma's going to give me a packet of tea leaves to take home with me."

Eve wrinkled her nose. She bit thoughtfully into a cake. "I had another dream," she said, "and there were dragons."

"Oh?"

"It was about that old teapot downstairs. The one Grandpa dug up in the garden." Derek noticed with annoyance that Eve was dropping crumbs all over his bedspread. "In my dream I was sitting high on a branch of the monkey puzzle tree, and the teapot floated over to me. I told it to go away but it wouldn't, and then, when I looked again, it was all gold, because it was magic, of course. There were these tiny dragons on it that were a hundred years old, and when I touched it the dragons flew away and spells came out of the top, like this." She made a loud whooshing noise.

"Very interesting," said Derek, feeling tired.

"Only special people dream about magic," said Eve, "and I'm one of them." Her eyes grew distant, and she slid off the bed, taking the crumbs with her. She drifted to the window. Snow was falling, blanketing up thickly against the house. "That's what the Ice Forest looks like," she murmured, turning in circles toward the door. "All covered in white." She spun around and around.

"Eve, you're making me dizzy."

"And you can hear the ice, like bells, tinkling in the wind. . . ."

She was gone. The wand lay on the bed, abandoned, its star crushed.

Derek sighed and pulled the towel over his head, breathing in the herbal steam.

After a time Grandma returned for the tea things.

"Feeling any better?" she asked.

"A bit," he replied.

"Must have caught a chill waiting for the bus, don't you think?" Grandma sat on the bed beside him. "But it's not really you I'm worried about, Derek," she said. "It's Eve."

"Oh?"

"She doesn't seem herself lately, I've noticed. I can't quite put my finger on it. Such a dreamy little thing,

with that wistful smile. She has a marvelous imagi-
nation, really, loves to pretend and all."

"Eve's sort of different from other kids," said Derek
hesitantly.

"She certainly is," chuckled Grandma. "Has a mind
of her own, that one. Oh, I don't say Eve can help
being one way or another. It's just a feeling I have."

"I think I know what you mean. She's so, well, unpredictable."

"Mmm," said Grandma. "One never knows with
Eve. She continually surprises us. I do worry some-
times." She stood up. Her apron was dusted with flour.
"There you go," she said, plumping up Derek's pillows.
"You should be a bit more comfy now. . . ."

Grandma piled up the tea tray and carried it to the
door. She turned back and caught Derek's gaze.
"You'll see no harm comes to Eve, won't you, Derek?"
she asked.

He nodded.

"There we are," she said with a smile. "I knew I
could rely on you." She closed the door behind her.

14

The Boy in the Storm

Derek was not allowed out of bed for three long days. After finishing *The Gorilla Hunters*, he went on to *Children of the New Forest*, and then a volume of frightening ghost stories, which he read by candlelight. Grandma warned him to be especially watchful of drafts and gave him Grandpa's old flannel bathrobe to wear about the house. Every four hours he was made to inhale one of Grandma's herbal concoctions from a huge blue mixing bowl. He spent hours lining tin soldiers along the windowsill, imagining great bloody battles on the hillsides of Wales. Sometimes Eve turned up for a game of dominoes or shyly presented him with one of her drawings.

Meanwhile, the storm raged outside.

After the third day Derek could stand it no more. Once everyone had gone to bed, he slipped into his clothes and away into the darkness. He felt wonderfully free, the wind smacking his face, snow falling like pale blossoms, as he cut a zigzag path up the Tumpy. The fire in Ashcroft's chamber, when Derek arrived, was nearly out.

Ashcroft did not look well. Feeling at once very awkward, Derek scuffed over to where he lay, shivering, beneath a ragged pile of blankets. Ashcroft peered out at him with dull, shadowy eyes. His face had thinned and aged, giving him the lean, scorched look of a desert prophet.

"I've had a fever," he told Derek. "Three, maybe four days. It came on quite suddenly."

"I'll make you something warm to drink," the boy offered, and set to work raking the coals in the dying hearth and putting the kettle to boil. Minutes later Derek returned to Ashcroft's side with two cups of tea and a box of arrowroot biscuits. "Isn't there anyone to look after you?" he asked.

"The Dreamkeepers come by from time to time, but they've had troubles of their own. The Usk Beetles, you see." He pulled himself up and looked hard at

Derek. "And yourself? Seems we haven't seen you in quite some time."

"I had the fever, too. I was on a bus, coming out of town, and Iona sat behind me. By the time Grandma got me into the house, I was delirious."

"It is a bad sign, illness," said Ashcroft.

They drank awhile in silence. Then Derek spoke. "But . . . I thought you never got sick, Mr. Ashcroft. I thought you were supposed to live . . ." his voice fell to a strangled whisper, ". . . forever?"

Ashcroft smiled weakly. "No one lives forever, lad. Though I daresay I may have a few good centuries left."

"Centuries?" Derek looked around the room. There was no telling how long it had been there. It seemed to be as old as any priory or castle he had ever seen.

"I'm glad you've come, I must say," said Ashcroft. "Now then. I would like to go back in time, to a winter's day many years ago, when a boy such as you, Derek, turned up at my door. It seems he had lost his way in a storm. Snowing like the devil, it was. I offered him shelter and a cup of tea. And, like you, he met the Dreamkeepers."

Chewing a stale biscuit, Derek listened thought-fully.

"There was one Dreamkeeper, Owain his name was, who had fallen very ill indeed. He lay on a pallet in the Hall of the Dreamkeepers and had not spoken a word for many days. When the boy entered the Hall, Owain sat suddenly up and pointed a shaky finger at him. For Owain knew, the moment he set eyes on the boy, that he was the one."

"The one what?" asked Derek.

"Why, the one sent to help us defeat Iona. Owain insisted the boy write down an ancient poem, one that described the location of a missing relic."

"What happened then?" asked Derek, enthralled.

"Unfortunately the boy did not fare well. Had he succeeded, Iona and the dark dreams would no longer exist."

"What happened to the boy?"

"Now then. I believe he took his copy of the poem with him, scrawled across a page of lined copy paper. His heart was heavy, I know, because he had failed, or so he believed. We never saw him again. Often, over the years, I have wondered what became of him. That is somewhat of a mystery, you see."

"Maybe he was afraid," said Derek in a small voice. "Maybe it was too scary for him."

"Perhaps. But I had hoped—for the boy would be an old man by now—that the poem still exists. Somewhere. How does such a story strike you, Derek Morgan?"

"Well, there is a box," Derek began, watching a faint spark of light appear at the back of Ashcroft's eyes. "It was Grandpa's when he was a boy, and he kept all sorts of junk inside, you know. And then . . . I found an old piece of paper, kind of yellow and crinkly, so I knew it was old, folded up inside the lid. . . ."

Ashcroft leaned forward expectantly. "And . . . ?"

"Well, I had a quick look at it. It was pretty messy, and the words were all jumbled together, but I knew it was something, well, important. Why else would he have saved it all those years?" He leaned back and closed his eyes, trying to work it all out. "It was the poem, wasn't it, Mr. Ashcroft? That's what you've been talking about. My grandpa was the boy who copied the verse."

"Yes," replied Ashcroft quietly. "Yes, he was."

"But why ask a boy? Why not ask a knight, or a baron? Why not ask the prime minister?"

"Ah, the knights are long gone, my lad, and the prime minister must deal with more pressing matters. The Morgans, you see, have been our allies longer than I can remember. They have stood by the Dream-keepers for centuries."

"They have? Really?" Derek was astounded: No one had ever told him his family went back centuries. He thought a moment. "Then I don't understand why you didn't ask my father. He lived here as a boy, and he's a Morgan. Why did you wait years and years for me to turn up?"

Ashcroft's face grew solemn. "Ah, but we did ask your father. We sent the Dreams to him countless times, but never once did he respond. We were puzzled at first, but then we realized he wasn't at all interested. He didn't believe in the Dreams, you see. His head was always filled with facts and theorems, and he had no time for fantasy. You could say he abandoned the Dreams."

Derek considered. His father was a practical sort, no doubt about it, forever going on about statistics and equations and logical proofs. "We had no choice but to wait," concluded Ashcroft. "Once we knew there was another Morgan in Rhydhowell, we sent out the Dreams, hoping you would make sense of them. Running on faith, we were."

"And I found you!"

"Indeed." Ashcroft sank back into the pillows, folding his long fingers. "And so, once again, the Dreamkeepers have hope."

15

Vanished

The box was gone.

Derek had looked everywhere, rummaging through drawers, shaking out the comforter, tearing the sheets from his bed. He was sure he'd left it beneath his pillow, yet he could find no sign of it. A box just couldn't vanish into thin air, he told himself. It made him ill to think he had lost it, and the poem inside as well. Was it possible that Iona had had something to do with this?

He crawled under his bed, discovering the Airfix modeling kit he had bought on his last visit to High Street, then crawled out again.

"What are you doing under there?" asked Eve from the doorway, wearing a fur coat that had once belonged to Cousin Gwennie. She looked like a small bear. "You've got cobwebs all over you."

Derek straightened up and brushed himself off. "I've lost something."

"I'll help you find it," offered Eve. She lifted up a game board and all the pieces went sliding off. "What are you looking for, anyway?"

"It doesn't matter," he said, disconsolate. "I don't want any help. I have this awful feeling it's gone for good."

"This room is *messy*," said Eve in a voice that made Derek want to hit her. "It's no good trying to find anything when there's all this junk. That's what Mom always says."

Derek pitched a comic at her, but Eve was already out the door.

The day passed uneventfully. Late in the afternoon Mr. Stewart Palethorpe dropped in for a cup of tea. A retired headmaster, he was fussy and prim and rolled his *r*'s. He told them that once a fortnight he took the express into London, where he scoured the back-street markets in search of Victorian porcelain. His specialty was thimbles. This endeared him to Grandma, who collected them herself.

Derek and Eve sat yawning and eating pastries

during the conversation. Eve wanted to know if Mr. Palethorpe ever ran across old dolls, or comic books maybe, but he just laughed his hiccupy laugh and never answered. Eve frowned at him over her glass of lemonade.

"Well, I rrreally must be off." With a nervous smile, Mr. Palethorpe unfolded himself from the couch and stood up. Everyone followed him into the hall, where he retrieved his coat and an extraordinarily large pair of galoshes.

"Ghastly weather, don't you think?" He peered through the frosted glass of the front door.

"Oh, Mr. Palethorpe, I nearly forgot." Grandma turned to Derek. "Run up, my dear, and fetch that little box of Grandpa's. You know the one I mean. Mr. Palethorpe was keen on having a look at it."

Derek went pale. "The box? You mean . . . the box?" His heart sank. "I'm sorry, Grandma, but it seems to have, well . . . vanished. I can't find it anywhere."

Grandma looked surprised. "Ah, there's a pity. Well, never mind, it's bound to turn up."

"Another day, then." Mr. Palethorpe pulled on the door and was nearly blown backward by a gust of wind. "Cheerio!" he called, and disappeared into the storm.

"Do you know anything about this missing box, Eve?" asked Grandma, looking stern.

"Me?" said Eve.

Derek glared at her. "If you've taken it. . . ." he said between clenched teeth.

"Don't get mad," Eve told him. "If you're talking about that tinny little box with the squiggles, I found it in the pantry next to the Weetabix."

"You did?" Grandma seemed confused.

"Uh-oh," said Derek. "Now I remember. I was looking for some metal polish. Somebody must have interrupted me or something, and I forgot all about it."

"Anyway," said Eve, "I've found a use for it."

"Eve," said Grandma, "tell us where it is."

"Oh, all right. Follow me, then." She led them into the kitchen, where she stooped down and reached behind the stove. "Here it is," she said, retrieving the box and handing it over to Derek.

He looked down at it suspiciously. "So what've you done with it?"

"Ssst, be quiet or you'll wake him up." Eve gently opened the box. Curled inside, fast asleep, was a small brown mouse.

Dropping the startled mouse into Eve's hand, Derek snatched the box, raced upstairs, and slammed the door behind him. He tipped the box, peering anxiously inside the lid.

The paper was still there.

In the middle of the night Derek awoke, shivering,

huddled at the foot of his bed beneath the blankets. He'd been having dreams again, dreams of fantastic ice-creatures chasing him across windblown fields of snow. All night they had pursued him, reaching out with fingers of ice. It was time, he knew: He could wait no longer. Bundling up in his warmest clothes, he set out for the Tumpy.

It was still dark when he arrived in the Hall of the Dreamkeepers. Hands trembling, he unfolded the yellow sheet of paper and gave it to Ashcroft. "This is the poem you told me about," he said, "the verse that Grandpa saved. Maybe the Dreamkeepers can figure out what it says."

"It is not for us to decipher the words," replied Ashcroft, gently handing it back. "The spell is yours to unravel."

"I can't read all those scribbles," Derek told him. "It's been written in some weird code."

One of the Dreamkeepers stepped forward. His beard trailed to his knees, and he looked as insubstantial as a dry leaf.

"This is the way of spells, not some riddle-game, boy," he said. "You must seek not only the words but the meaning beyond them. For this is the path of light that leads to enchantment."

The Dreamkeepers crowded around Derek, and he felt as though he were seeing them for the first time.

He realized how fragile they really were, how transitory. They were like an endangered species, doomed to extinction.

His mouth felt papery and dry. "All right," he said, "if that's how it is. Let's get on with it."

There was a murmur of approval, and the Dreamkeepers returned to their books. Ashcroft led Derek to a chair beside the fire.

"The Usk Beetles were here last night," Ashcroft told him. "I am certain that Iona suspects we are up to something."

Derek sat and stared at the verse. He folded it, then unfolded it, smoothing it out on the arm of the chair. It was like trying to work out some impossible equation.

"Hmm," he said, "let's see, now. . . ." He turned the paper upside down. He might as well be trying to read Tasmanian. Meanwhile, Ashcroft paced nervously up and down the Hall, while the Dreamkeepers brewed endless pots of tea.

"Don't worry," the Elder Dreamkeeper reassured Ashcroft. "He's from the line of Morgans, isn't he? Have faith the boy knows what he's about."

"Yes, of course, I know that," muttered Ashcroft, and resumed his pacing.

Derek closed his eyes and ran his fingers over the

words like a blind person, trying to extract their meaning. It was giving him a headache.

"Um . . . Mr. Ashcroft?" he said, looking up. The piercing green eyes met his. "Maybe I need some more light."

A Dreamkeeper rose from the table. "Perhaps this will do," she said, holding up the orb of the Llanellith. Derek turned to see the Dreamkeeper step lightly in his direction. Very carefully, she placed the globe on a table beside him.

"Thanks," said Derek, and he looked down at the paper. It was as if a handful of tiny stars had been thrown across its surface. The letters seemed to dance in the light, cartwheeling across the page. He looked again and saw they had turned into words, ones he could recognize.

At length Derek said softly, "Mr. Ashcroft?"

The Dreamkeepers dropped their quill pens and looked up. Ashcroft raked the last few embers in the hearth and rose to his feet.

"I—I think I've got it figured out now," said Derek. Beside the dying fire, he quietly recited:

"Through storm and tunnel the boy must travel
If this spell he shall unravel.
A journey by night through deepening snow,

Then far to the Other Side he will go.
In darkness it lies, and yet in full view,
Disguised by time, and the dreams of a few.
To the touch it is hot, yet other times cold,
The color of earth, the sparkle of gold."

Derek slowly folded the paper and put it back into his pocket. He hadn't a clue what any of it meant.

16

The Path of Enchantment

There was a door, said Ashcroft, that led to what the Dreamkeepers called the Other Side. The Elder Dreamkeeper showed Derek the way. They passed from the Great Hall into a long, narrow room. Here books were piled high on desks, their bindings torn, the pages riddled with holes. At the far end was a door hewn of thick wood, with a wrought-iron latch. A corner of the door had been gnawed away, proof that the Usk Beetles had been there before him.

"Keep the verse in mind, for it describes the object you must bring back," said the Elder Dreamkeeper in a voice like the flutter of moth wings. She handed Derek a lantern. A pale light flickered inside its glass orb. "Take care the lantern does not crack, or fall. Should the glass be broken . . ." Her voice dwindled into silence.

He flung open the door. Darkness lay beyond.

"Have you memorized the verse?"

"I did, except, um. . . ." Derek's voice faltered. "I don't really understand it. What am I supposed to be looking for?"

"You will know soon enough," the Dreamkeeper assured him. "Through that door lies the path of enchantment and understanding. When the light begins to fail, you must return."

Derek nodded, trying hard to feel brave.

There was nothing more to say. He stood in the doorway and felt as if he were poised at the edge of the galaxy. He set off down the tunnel with slow, loping strides. A sharp wind struck his face. As the tunnel curved, he picked up speed, and before long he was out of breath. He began to regret all those second helpings of pudding and scones.

Before long he reached a junction where three tunnels met. He veered to the left and kept going. Other junctions followed, and always he turned to the left, instinctively, picking up speed as he raced through the darkness. Time seemed to be measured in heartbeats and the thump of his boots on the tunnel floors.

At last he came to a door of unpainted wood, with rusted hinges and a clear glass knob. He hesitated a moment, then boldly pushed it open and peered inside. The lantern threw eerie shadows across stone walls and a dirt floor. He felt a stab of disappointment as he realized this was an ordinary cellar, nothing more.

He hurried through the cellar and up a stairway to another door. This one opened onto a narrow hallway. Derek held up the lamp, illuminating a coatrack, a cabinet of knickknacks, an umbrella stand. At the far end was a door, its window glazed with frost. Somewhere a clock ticked loudly.

A ghostly face swam up before him, and he jumped, then recognized his own reflection in a mirror. Heart pounding, he leaned against the cabinet. At the edge of his vision he saw something familiar. Thimbles? He held the light to the glass door for a closer look. Lined up in tidy little rows were Grandma's thimbles! Why, there was the blue-and-white Dutch thimble he'd given her one Christmas, the one with the windmill.

He wheeled around. It didn't make sense! Why would the path of enchantment lead to his grandparents' house?

He turned toward the living room. Well, why not, he reasoned: Hadn't Ashcroft told him the Morgans were special, that for centuries they'd battled enemies of the Dreamkeepers? Hadn't they sent Grandpa on a similar quest? He moved cautiously about the room, careful not to upset anything, inspecting vases and figurines. "The color of earth, the sparkle of gold . . ." He recited the verse like an incantation as he lifted up a wooden goblet.

There were geometric designs along the rim, and the carved wood was earth-colored. It felt cool in his hands. This could be it! He ran to the door but then stopped midway. "To the touch it is hot, yet other times cold." How could a wine goblet ever be hot?

Reluctantly he set it back on the table.

Next he charged into the kitchen and peered into the pantry. There were all sorts of cans and boxes here: cocoa and lemon curd, oxtail soup and baby butter beans. Sage-and-onion stuffing mix. "In darkness it lies, and yet in full view," he murmured, feeling his throat tighten: This was too hard. How could he figure out the riddle when the words were so abstract?

Darkness . . . He turned slowly, then raced over and flung open the refrigerator door. It was always dark in here, he thought, as long as the door was closed. Inside he found two boiled eggs, a wedge of cheese, and a packet of sliced tongue. He reached for an egg: cold, but hot when first boiled. Its brown shell was the color of earth. And it was golden at the center. This is it, he told himself, cradling the egg in his hand.

Or was it? Who ever saw a yolk sparkle? Crestfallen, he replaced it and shut the refrigerator door.

Dejected, Derek returned to the hall, clumping upstairs to his room, Grandpa's old room. This was his last chance to set things right, he told himself, tears welling up behind his eyes. But this just seemed a meaningless treasure hunt that led nowhere.

The light within the lantern was growing dimmer.

As usual his bedroom was in chaos: shirts, socks, and pajamas strewn across the floor, along with books, chocolate wrappers, airplane kits, plastic dinosaurs. He waded through the mess to his dresser, tripping over a stack of games. He set the lantern beside a small stuffed alligator. It gazed blankly at him with cold glass eyes, and in the dim light its scales glittered like gold. Hurry, he told himself, you've got to find it! Frantically he tossed pillows and blankets into the air.

The alligator seemed to be smiling at him.

He rattled a box of inch-high brigadiers, then shook out a pencil case: Coins, stones, and souvenir pins spilled across the bed. His Tigers baseball hat fell to the floor. There was nothing that fit the verse. He snatched up the lantern and leaped over a chair, knocking his Monopoly board and sending the hotels flying. He yanked opened his bureau drawers, stirring up the clothes inside. Slam! Open, slam! Open, slam!

The alligator tumbled unnoticed to the floor.

Derek clattered back downstairs to the hall. Maybe he was being too logical: The Dreamkeeper had said to look for meaning beyond the words. "Disguised by time, and the dreams of a few . . ." What did it mean by time? And which dreams?

"It's no use," he said, and suddenly felt cold. He thought of the coal fire and entered the dining room. Only a few embers burned behind the grate. The lantern light was dying. "I've got to get back," he said aloud to the teapot on the mantle: the old leaky teapot, full of dents and scratches. He reached out with a finger and touched it.

The surface felt like ice.

"The teapot!" he gasped, suddenly remembering Eve's dream. The teapot was enchanted, Eve had said. Filled with spells, it had floated to her as she'd sat in the monkey puzzle tree. And it had turned the color of gold. Derek drew in a deep breath. "This is it," he whispered, "the teapot!"

Excitedly he grasped the handle, then fled the dining room, running through the hallway to the basement door, plunging back into the darkness of the cellar. He had no idea how much time had gone by, but he knew he must return soon. Ashcroft and the Dreamkeepers were waiting on the far side of the tunnel, wondering if they'd ever see him again, possibly fearing the worst.

The cellar closed in around him: He groped for the door, found the knob, opened it. His breath came in ragged puffs as he raced down the maze of corridors. His legs felt leaden, but he kept going, bracing himself against a freezing wind. It didn't matter, he told himself; nothing mattered now—he had the teapot!

Then, behind the wind, he heard another sound, a distant crunching.

As he ran the crunching grew louder. Suddenly Usk Beetles swarmed around him, flinging themselves at his back, his face, and at the dented teapot. He tried to outrun them, hoping to lose them at each turn, but more kept coming, swirling and buzzing, clinging to his sleeves and jacket, wings beating against the glass orb of the lantern.

"Ashcroft!" he yelled wildly.

Struggling up a long, curving slope, he saw a pale rectangle of light just ahead. Figures appeared within a doorway. "Ashcroft!" he yelled again as the teapot grew warmer, its handle burning in his hand. Light streamed from the open door into the blackness. Fearful of the light, the Usk Beetles rose in confused alarm. With angry metallic sounds, they reversed direction and swarmed back down the tunnel.

Derek lurched forward, then fell, landing in a web of wiry arms.

17

The Riddle Solved

Derek lay motionless on the stone floor. An unearthly golden light filled the room. He wondered if perhaps he was in heaven.

Looking up he saw the Dreamkeepers, hovering above him like wise, beaming angels. Derek winced and hoisted himself onto his elbows. Next to him lay the teapot, the source of the eerie light.

"It was Eve's dream—" he began, but all eyes were fixed on the teapot. As they watched, awestruck, the handle suddenly curved higher, looping into a sleek arc. Waves of light rippled across its surface; then the light grew so strong that Derek flinched and looked away. When he looked again, the teapot had become still, transformed into a vessel of shining gold.

"It is the ancient teapot," explained Ashcroft. "Handed down over the centuries, it has belonged always to the Dreamkeepers. When Iona took over the tower of Rhonabwy Court, the teapot vanished from sight. No one knew where it had gone."

Derek scrambled to his feet. The Dreamkeepers stood in a cluster, smiling and nodding, transfixed by the sight of the teapot.

Tugging on Ashcroft's sleeve, Derek asked, with a quiver in his voice, "When Grandpa went down the tunnel . . . where exactly did it take him?"

"The tunnel in fact led Rhys deep underground," came the reply. "Iona had hidden the teapot there, thinking we would never find it."

"But is—" began Derek. "The tunnel *is* real, isn't it?"

"Ah, but there is more than one tunnel, you see. Beneath the hills of Rhydhowell run scores of underground corridors. They lead to what the Dreamkeepers call the Other Side—the world beyond Rhonabwy Court. The tunnels have always been there; certain ones were first used centuries ago when the Morgans joined forces with the Dreamkeepers. They may be entered only through the power of the Dreamkeepers, a venture not without risk—as well you know."

"What happened to Grandpa then?"

"Sad to say, young Rhys dropped the teapot somewhere in one of the tunnels on his way back," explained Ashcroft. "With the Usk Beetles at his heels, there was no returning for it."

"He had an idea where the teapot had landed," said a Dreamkeeper. "He knew it lay someplace beneath the hillside."

"Who knows how many years he had been digging before finding it again," commented another.

No wonder his grandfather had never wanted to move, thought Derek. Rhys Morgan had spent nearly sixty years searching for the lost teapot!

"Listen now, Derek," said Ashcroft, guiding him away from the others. "The time has come to make our move against Iona." His voice carried a sudden sense of great urgency.

Derek nodded.

"The plan is simple enough," continued Ashcroft. "The teapot, you see, is the most ancient of relics, and contains certain powers—powers strong enough to destroy Iona. It has never failed us. The first step is to brew tea in the teapot, then offer a cup to Iona. She need only take a single sip—" he paused, tugging thoughtfully at his beard—"and the dark dreams will exist no more."

Derek felt a faint stirring of dread. "How will we ever do that?" he asked, avoiding Ashcroft's piercing gaze.

"There is only one individual Iona trusts, and that is your sister. It is a gamble, of course, but Eve must somehow convince Iona to take that sip."

"And if something goes wrong?" Derek asked uncertainly.

"Let us not talk of failure," said Ashcroft, his eyes hardening. He grasped the shining teapot in his hands and strode off to join the others.

In the bleak light of early morning Derek trudged wearily down the Tumpy to his grandparents' house. Here and there a stray snowflake spun down from the sky. He was halfway through the garden when he noticed Grandpa leaning in the doorway, smoking a pipe.

"More snow to come, they say," said Grandpa in a dry voice, following Derek inside the house. "Been off on another adventure, have you?"

"Sort of," mumbled Derek, slinging his jacket onto the back of a chair.

"That will drip," warned Grandpa. "Hang it on the rack beside the fire."

In the dining room Derek avoided looking at the empty space on the mantel where the teapot had been.

"Seems we had an intruder in the night," said Grandpa from the doorway. "Bit of a bungled job, I'd say. He made off with that old teapot I dug up last summer."

"Really?" said Derek, trying to show only faint interest. "That's strange."

"It's strange indeed," agreed Grandpa, hobbling back to the kitchen. He slid a tray of sliced bread under the grill.

"What sort of madness would possess a bloke to come in here and take that dented old thing?" Grandpa went on, breaking eggs into a bowl. "Wouldn't even fetch a fiver, I reckon."

Derek chewed on his lower lip. "Maybe he was new at burgling," he suggested lamely.

"Hmmph." Grandpa stirred the eggs fiercely. "The world is a funny old place," he mused. "No telling what will come of that teapot. Blasted thing could turn up at Sotheby's auction room and fetch a small fortune."

"What if . . . what if whoever took it had a good reason?" asked Derek impulsively, his face flushing bright red.

"A good reason, you say?" Rhys Morgan yanked out the tray of toast and eyed his grandson warily. Then his gaze softened. "What you mean is, perhaps the teapot was needed elsewhere, for something important?"

Derek nodded sheepishly.

Grandpa's stern face suddenly folded into a smile. "Right, then. Best not to mention any of this to Grandma, eh?" He poured the eggs into the pan. "I'll tell her I've lent it to old Palethorpe."

Derek relaxed suddenly and smiled back.

Grandpa's face grew solemn again. "Just take my advice, will you lad, and keep your wits about you."

Derek nodded gravely, the image of young Rhys Morgan flashing vividly before him. There were so many questions he wanted to ask, but perhaps they were best left unspoken.

The kitchen door swung open and Grandma bustled in. "Fancy you two up so early," she said, waving out the window to the milkman. "And breakfast almost ready. Quite a team, you are!"

Derek and his grandfather exchanged conspiratorial grins. Then, whistling softly, Rhys Morgan returned to his eggs.

18

Midnight Tea

After breakfast Derek and Eve sat drawing at the dining room table. Snow flurried against the windows, and from time to time the wind gave a long, hollow moan.

Derek had sketched a map of the Tumpy with his calligraphy pen. It was really pretty good, he thought, as he shaded in Rhonabwy Court. "This map," he said, holding it up, "could save our lives. We'll never get lost on the Tumpy again if we bring this with us."

"*I* never got lost on the Tumpy," Eve said in a prickly voice. "You did." She chewed on the eraser of her pencil. "Anyway, a map won't help us. There'll be too much snow. Iona told me it's never going to stop."

Derek's eyes narrowed. "What else did Iona tell you?"

"She promised to take me to see the seals." Eve's eyes were shadowed and her face flushed. "They live in the Ice Forest, and only Iona has ever seen them."

Derek flicked his pen against the table edge, wondering how to convince Eve to agree to Ashcroft's plan. Time was running out.

"Did Iona ever tell you about the teapot of spells?" he asked. "It was lost a long time ago, and it's extremely valuable."

Eve looked up. "What kind of spells?"

"Powerful ones," he said in a voice he hoped sounded authoritative. "Some so strong they could turn the entire world into a forest of ice."

"That would be brilliant!" said Eve. "Then I could live in one of those snow caves."

"Do y'think Iona would want it?"

"Want what?" Eve rubbed the eraser so hard that it made holes in her paper.

"You're not listening," said Derek. "I think we should go to Rhonabwy Court tonight. You could surprise Iona with a nice cup of tea."

"That sounds boring," said Eve obstinately, and began packing up her box of colored pencils. "Besides, Iona hates surprises."

"We could take Grandpa's old rucksack and pack sandwiches and jam tarts. I'll bring this map so we don't get lost. It'll be a real adventure."

"Banana sandwiches?" Eve closed the box of pencils and studied her drawing thoughtfully. "Well, maybe." She stood up, spilling half her pencils on the floor. Her eyes seemed to be clouded, as though she were falling into some kind of trance.

"Eve?"

The dining room door banged softly shut. Derek looked over at Eve's drawing. It was of a house with rows of windows and a tower on top. She's fudged the monkey puzzle tree, he thought. Looking more closely, he saw a face in the tower. It was the face of a small girl, trapped inside.

The rucksack thumped against Derek's back as he and Eve followed the white-arched path up the Tumpy. Their boots crunched over the crisp snow, while flakes fell around them in endless slanting patterns.

As they neared the clearing, a shower of loose snow fell from a branch down the back of Derek's neck. He shivered: It was hard to feel brave in the night, when the dark, silent mountains made him feel so small and powerless.

Buried in snow, the monkey puzzle tree stood guard

over Rhonabwy Court like a great phantom pyramid. Derek slowed down as he approached the tree. From beneath the convoluted branches stepped a Dreamkeeper. Without a word she handed over the teapot, wrapped in a velvet cloth. Taking it, he swallowed hard, trying to muffle the empty feeling in his throat.

Eve, meanwhile, had fallen into a drift and was scrambling out of the deep snow. "Who was that?" she gasped, running to catch up with Derek. "The person in the long robe? Who was it?" She lifted a branch of the tree and looked beneath it, but the Dreamkeeper had vanished.

"Oh, nobody special," replied Derek, trying to sound casual. "One of Mr. Ashcroft's librarians, that's all." The last thing he wanted was to arouse Eve's suspicions.

Inside the kitchen at Rhonabwy Court, Derek set to work at once, filling the kettle with water and setting it on the range. He placed the teapot, still covered, on the counter. Next he flipped open the straps of the rucksack, scattering the contents across the patterned oilcloth on the table. Out spilled a box of matches, his map, two candles, sandwiches wrapped in foil, jam tarts, and a packet of Grandma's best tea.

"My banana sandwich is all squashed," complained Eve as she tore off the foil. "It looks horrible."

"You can have mine," said Derek, unable to shake

the hollow feeling. "I'm not hungry." He lit the candles and placed them in saucers, then struck another match and lit the burner.

Next he removed the cloth from the teapot and set it on the table. Eve fell silent and for a long moment just stared. "It's the one from my dream!" she gasped. "The teapot full of spells!"

Derek nodded, standing back to admire its glimmering light.

"I told you it was enchanted," he said matter-of-factly, shaking tea leaves into the pot.

Eve picked up the empty tea packet and studied it briefly. "Tea's boring. Why do people in Wales drink it all the time?"

Derek added hot water to the leaves and stirred. "Grandpa says drinking tea is a national pastime."

Suddenly Eve froze, listening intently. "Someone's coming," she whispered, her face turning pale. "Iona!"

"Right, then," said Derek. Suddenly the hairs on the back of his neck crawled, and his palms went clammy. Hand shaking, he poured the tea, then shoved the cup at Eve. "Here, take it. After she's taken a sip, you can tell her about the teapot, but not before."

Eve nodded, wriggling with excitement. Tea sloshed onto the saucer as she carried the cup gingerly into the dim, echoing room that adjoined the kitchen. With its magnificent leaded windows and parquet floor, it had once been the dining hall of Rhonabwy Court. Now it contained only cobwebs and empty bookshelves.

Derek hid behind the kitchen door. This is all just a game to Eve, he thought ruefully, and watched as Iona sailed ominously into view.

Eve stood at the center of the room, holding out the cup of tea. A thin curl of steam rose into the air.

"For me, is it?" Iona said frostily. She wore a dark, hooded gown and her hair was unpinned, falling to her shoulders like bristly eels.

"It's piping hot," said Eve proudly, handing the cup to Iona.

"I should hope so," Iona replied loftily. "There is nothing so dreadful as cold tea." She lifted the cup to her lips, then paused.

Take a sip, Derek pleaded silently. Just one. He could see Eve through the crack in the door, a smile flickering at the corners of her mouth.

"You must tell me what you find so amusing." Iona's voice was sharp as glass as she set the cup back in its saucer. "I cannot tolerate secrets and, in particular, *children's* secrets."

Eve looked down, fiddling with the buttons on her jacket.

Iona lifted the cup to her lips and sniffed. Derek

froze as the outside door opened and Zylar tramped in, shaking his red scarf. He held his breath as Zylar set a bundle of wood next to the stove, flung his scarf over the table, and continued on into the dining hall.

"Is something wrong?" inquired Zylar, creaking over to Iona.

"This tea smells peculiar."

Frowning, Zylar peered into the cup. "Smells like old socks," he said.

"It's a surprise," said Eve meekly, and hung her head.

Derek felt his stomach twist in a fresh panic. He gripped the edge of the kitchen door.

"You promised you'd take me to the Ice Forest." Eve gave a small hiccup. "You said over and over you would."

Narrowing her silver eyes, Iona said, "I don't quite follow."

"I thought if you had the teapot you'd take me there."

Iona's eyes took on a wild, combustible look "Teapot? What teapot?" She held the cup at arm's length and let go. Zylar jumped as it shattered on the wooden floor.

"I know of only one teapot," said Iona in a quiet, seething voice, "and that one lies far underground, lost in a tunnel well over sixty year ago. Unless some fool—" She pivoted on her heels and stormed toward the kitchen. "Where is the teapot?"

With a thin cry, Derek spun around and flew into the pantry. He looked wildly about and, spotting a wooden crate, clambered in. Reaching up, he clawed at a sack of vegetables, groaning as the heavy bundle landed on top of him.

From the kitchen, meanwhile, came a terrible racket. He could hear Iona shouting and Eve crying. There was a heart-stopping silence, then a deafening crash that left him stunned.

The teapot!

"Who put you up to this?" he heard Iona shout. "Where is that devious brother of yours, I want to know! And that tuppenny-ha'penny magician?"

She was answered only by uncontrollable sobbing.

"The boy can't be far," rasped Zylar, kicking open the pantry door. "I know you're in here!" he snarled, pushing aside a sack of onions.

Derek hugged his knees and curled into a ball. He heard a box tumble to the floor, baskets overturning, the sound of glass bottles breaking.

"Don't play silly games with me," Zylar warned. He cursed loudly as more objects went flying. A barrel of flour tipped, and the cursing gave way to a violent sneezing.

"Forget the boy, he's long gone," hissed Iona from the doorway.

"Sniveling rat!" Giving the barrel an extra kick, Zylar retreated.

Derek waited as the voices faded and died away. There was a long, breathless silence. He extracted himself from under the sack and climbed stiffly out of the crate. The air was thick with flour. Dazed, he stumbled into the kitchen. When he saw the teapot, the hollow pain in his throat suddenly returned.

It lay on its side next to the iron stove. Its magnificent surface was pitted and scratched, its lid badly dented; in the dim kitchen its golden hues had turned a dull shade of rust. From the twisted spout came a thin trickle of tea, forming a dark pool on the stone floor. Pincers raised, scores of Usk Beetles scuttled from beneath the stove and cabinet; others peered out from cracks in the walls. They trundled toward the teapot. Soon they had surrounded it completely.

Derek backed away uncertainly. There wasn't time now to decide what to do about the teapot. Iona had taken Eve . . . where? He raced madly through the frozen rooms of Rhonabwy Court until he came to the foot of the main staircase. A handful of star-shaped flakes drifted past him. He stood gazing up, unable to believe his eyes: Down the turned staircase snow was falling, strange dreamlike patterns drifting down the long flight of steps.

19

Rhonabwy Court under Siege

Deep underground in the Great Hall, the Dream-keepers huddled beside the fire, though its flames gave scarcely any warmth. Dagger-shaped icicles had begun to appear on the rafters overhead. The pages of the worn leather-bound books were frozen shut, and ice had formed inside the glass bottles of ink. It was just after midnight when Derek returned. Ashcroft rose to his feet as the boy stumbled into the room, snow billowing behind him. The Dreamkeepers rose together in the dying light.

Derek looked around. "Iona wouldn't drink the tea,"

he told them. Angrily he tore off his jacket and threw it down. "Iona bullied Eve until she told her about the teapot, then she flew into a rage and—" Wordlessly he flung his mittens across the room.

There was silence all around.

"The teapot has failed us," said a Dreamkeeper in a leaden voice.

"I never thought such a thing could happen," murmured another.

Derek began to shiver. "W-why is it so c-cold?" he asked. His breath hung suspended in the bone-chilling air. A mug of tea appeared in his hands, and he took a long, noisy drink, wiping his nose at intervals. "I think they've gone up to the tower," he said, looking up bleakly at Ashcroft. "I came back for you."

Ashcroft nodded, handing a woolen cloak to Derek. This was followed by a pair of dry mittens. "The temperature is falling," he murmured. When Derek was ready, Ashcroft tossed him a small ice pick. "This may prove useful as well."

The Great Hall seemed to grow colder by the minute. "Well, then," said Ashcroft, unhooking the lantern from its place by the hearth. "It is time."

"But . . ." Derek paused, looking back at the Dreamkeepers. They stood shivering, blinking their green eyes at him, their faces pinched and ill-looking. He could see beneath their robes the knobbly outlines of their twig-shaped bones. "Aren't they coming with us?"

"Their strength is ebbing, I'm afraid," said Ashcroft, steering Derek through the arch. "They haven't much time left."

Derek held the lantern as they moved swiftly down the black, winding tunnels. He couldn't help thinking about the other Dreamkeepers, locked in Iona's spell of ice. Were all of them doomed? Ashcroft navigated through the frozen darkness, opening a door that led up a creaking staircase.

Fresh snow sifted over them as they neared the top of the stairs.

"What's the plan?" Derek asked quietly. "Do we storm the tower?"

"We've no choice, really, have we?" said Ashcroft grimly.

They entered the third-floor corridor. Derek lifted the lantern high, staring at the tangled cobwebs overhead. They glittered eerily. "The cobwebs have all turned to ice," he whispered, and followed Ashcroft to the end of the hallway. There was an expectant silence. They moved cautiously to the final door.

"I'll go on ahead," offered Derek, looking around uneasily. There was a faint ringing in his ears, low and threatening. Warily he edged up the steps and peered into the tower.

Candles burned in the iron hoop, throwing violet shadows across the room. Icicles hung like great jagged teeth from the wooden rafters, and frost glazed the arched windows. The floor gleamed like a sheet of dark glass.

No one was there.

Derek called back to Ashcroft. Slamming the door behind him, Ashcroft drew the bolt and leaned against the door, breathing hard.

"What happens when Iona comes back?" asked Derek nervously.

"It is a simple matter now," said Ashcroft, stepping away from the door. "It is a test of strength that she can never win. This tower belongs to the Dreamkeepers, and has for centuries." He took the lantern from Derek, set it on the glassy floor, then drew himself tall and erect. "Iona will *not* win. I shall see to that."

From a far corner of the room, where snow had gathered in great rounded heaps, came a faint, scuttering sound.

"Usk Beetles?" whispered Derek.

Then they heard the far-off croaking of Eve's voice: "Is that you, Derek?"

Derek picked his way across the icy floor to the drifts and knelt down. In one of them a cave had been hollowed out, and under a stack of blankets sat Eve, cross-legged, squinting at him blindly like a mole.

"Eve! Are you all right?"

"I'm so c-cold," she said, her voice sounding far away. "And the dreams, they're all around—" Her face crumpled, and she began to cry.

"Don't think about the dreams, Eve. Everything's all right now," he said with a confidence he didn't feel. "I'll bet the Dreamkeepers are on their way this very minute."

"But I can't see!" she wailed. Tiny crystals of tears froze to her cheeks and lashes.

"The dark dreams, Derek!" Ashcroft gasped behind him, his face stricken with pain. "The room is filling with them. I don't think I can—" He doubled over.

"No!" cried Derek, sliding over the ice to Ashcroft. "Don't let the dark dreams in!"

"It's difficult to move," said Ashcroft. "And it's gone so very, very cold. . . ." His voice grew fainter. "Derek, listen. I was wrong to leave the teapot behind, to think it had failed us completely. You must bring the teapot here, to the tower." His voice faded. "Only then . . ." He sank to his knees.

"Don't give up now!" Derek shouted. "Think of heat, and summer, think of lizards sunning on the rocks!"

Ashcroft lifted one arm. It remainded in midair, frozen in place.

"Think of camels in the desert!" shrieked Derek. "The Sphinx!"

From the outside corridor came the sound of an axe, and wood as it splintered and broke apart. The locked door trembled.

"The Dreamkeepers!" cried Derek. "They've made it to the tower!"

With a thunderous crash, the door fell inward.

The flame inside the lantern flickered and died as the tower grew strangely still. Through the ruined entrance a shadow, archaic and forbidding, slowly made its way, staring at them with fierce, glittering eyes.

20

The Tower of Dark Dreams

Iona loomed forbiddingly over them, a tall, dark shadow that looked for a moment like some strange creature of the night. Her cloak swirled around her bare feet in the icy wind. Derek and Ashcroft exchanged anguished looks; Eve retreated into her snow cave. The candles seemed to wheel overhead, the walls tilted, and despair filled the tower.

"And who are you, to intrude in *my* tower? Prying, sniveling boy! And *you*!" Iona stared at Ashcroft with bemused silver eyes. "Playing childish games with teapots."

Ashcroft did not answer.

"You will find, Eve Morgan, that I am the only one you can trust," said Iona, tilting her chin arrogantly. She gave a silvery laugh as her bare feet moved soundlessly across the floor. "Now then. We will leave the moment Zylar arrives." She sat down in the spindle-backed chair.

Eve crawled reluctantly out from the snow cave.

"Are we really going to the Ice Forest?" she asked.

"Don't listen, Eve!" whispered Derek, but his words sounded oddly garbled. He gazed up at the hoop of burning candles, yet they quickly grew blurred and distant. When he opened his mouth again, he was unable to utter a word. A chilling numbness had set into his limbs, and even his bones felt cold.

Minutes ticked by. A drop of hot wax fell, landing on the back of Derek's hand. He started, woken from his strange reverie, and looked over at Iona. She was leaning forward, deep in conversation with Eve. Seeing his chance, Derek edged away, tiptoeing across the ice. Then he broke into a run, leaping down the steps and into the corridor.

Plunging down the main staircase, he tumbled headlong into the snow, rolling down the swelling drifts.

Breathless, Derek staggered into the kitchen. Snow

was falling here as well, and the room seemed ghostly and abandoned. The candles he had left burning on the table were gone, Zylar's scarf had vanished, and the teapot was nowhere to be seen.

He checked the glass cabinet, finding only saucers and a few cracked cups. "It's got to be here somewhere. . . ." he muttered, falling to his knees and groping beneath the new-fallen snow. Desperate, he gathered the snow up in armfuls, flinging it over his head.

Then he stopped. There was a faint but steady hum, originating somewhere below the kitchen table. Flopping onto his stomach, he peered underneath: The teapot was there, surrounded by Usk Beetles.

As Derek reached in with one mittened hand and grabbed hold, the humming escalated to a frenzied whine. He slowly dragged the teapot away, using his free hand to sweep aside the beetles. Enraged, they swarmed around his head, buzzing and crunching.

Derek tucked the teapot beneath one arm and set off through the frozen rooms of the first floor. Snow was coming down harder now; needle-sharp bits of ice pelted his face. When he reached the bottom of the staircase, he gripped the banister and leaned into the wind. His mittens were soaked; the ends of his fingers felt frozen. He started up, like an old-timer from another century, heading toward doom through the false, bright snow.

Flakes the size of Usk Beetles swirled around him. They *were* Usk Beetles.

Why fight them? said a voice inside his head. *Why don't you rest awhile? Lie down in the snow. . . .*

Bracing himself against the wind, Derek thought of his Aunt Ethel's farm, the endless fields of corn, the pesky flies, the year of the heat wave when the crops dried up and Uncle Mart's cows keeled over.

He passed the second floor. The banister creaked ominously, as if ready to snap under the weight of the ice. Twice he nearly toppled backward in the bitter wind.

At long last he came to the third floor. Battling more drifts, Derek made his way to the end of the corridor. As he approached the tower door, he stopped, confused: The door was somehow distorted, absurdly out of reach. With astonishment, he realized he could go no farther: The door was trapped behind a vast expanse of ice.

21

The Strange Fate of Iona

Derek's surprise turned to anger as he gazed at the barrier of ice, several feet thick, that blocked the tower door. It would take him all night to break through that! And by then it would be too late. . . .

There must be another way, he thought, shivering, as he tried to recall his first visit to the tower. He remembered vaguely a second door, with mullioned windows and a balcony beyond, which he had passed on the way to the tower door. Pulling off his mittens, he ran the tips of his fingers along the corridor wall, where the ice was thin. He slipped the pick from his jacket and tapped tentatively. The ice shattered easily. He struck harder and it splintered, falling in pieces at his feet.

Then beneath the pick rang the sound of metal: a latch of some sort, followed by mullioned windows and the grained wood of a door. He gave a few kicks, then rammed his shoulder against it. The door sprang open, and he stumbled onto a small balcony.

The cold air took his breath away, and a brisk wind sent currents of snow whirling. Derek leaned over the scrolled railing and looked down. Far below he could see the monkey puzzle tree, no larger than one of Eve's dollhouse toys. It made him dizzy just looking at it.

There was twenty feet of steep roof between where he stood and the tower. *Too far*, said a voice, Iona's voice. *You'll never make it.* But he pushed the voice from his mind and hoisted himself over the rail, eyes fixed on the glazed windows of the tower. Take your time, he told himself, inching crabwise across the slippery tiles. Snow lashed at his face and neck, and from time to time he stopped, blinded by the flurries or halted by a sudden gust of wind. As he drew nearer the tower, there was a loud clattering behind him: ice, he guessed, or loose tiles, falling from the roof. He didn't dare look back, but slid over the ice-encrusted roof with fierce concentration, aware of the tower just ahead, maddeningly out of reach.

Fearful of losing his grip, he held the teapot tighter, trying not to think of the beetles, or of the terrible distance between himself and the lawn below. When he finally grasped the ironwork that encircled the tower, something sharp stung his cheek. An Usk Beetle!

Reaching out cautiously, he tapped on the glass. A shadow moved back and forth behind the frosted panes.

The window creaked, then slowly opened. Spidery fingers moved swiftly toward him.

With a fearful cry, Derek pushed away Iona's hand and hurtled over the sill and through the open window, shouting, "Ashcroft, Ashcroft! I've got the teapot!"

There was a terrible silence.

"Ashcroft?" His heart slammed crazily against his ribs as he scrambled to his feet. "Eve?" The tower was filled with snow.

"You've come too late," said Iona, her face impassive.

Fear pricked at the bones of Derek's spine. His whole body began shaking as he looked wildly about the room. All he could see was snow, drifting up against the windows, swirling around the candles, blotting out the corners of the tower. The snow cave was gone, the spindled chair a blurred outline. Ashcroft and Eve were nowhere to be seen.

"Where are they?" he screamed.

There was only the wind, punctuated by the sound of Usk Beetles as they struck the windowpanes. Then, quite suddenly, they discovered the open window. With a frenetic beating of wings, they poured into the tower. Derek watched, terrified, as they circled ominously overhead. "Get away!" he cried, turning to run and slipping on the ice. The Usk Beetles flew straight at him.

Like a knight with his shield thrust forward, Derek flung the teapot before him with both arms. He shut his eyes tightly, flinching again and again as the Usk Beetles struck savagely against the metal. Then he noticed the teapot was growing warm in his hands. Opening one eye, he saw light flashing from its surface: brilliant and golden, bursting forth like a magnificent flame. The beetles faltered in the glare and seemed to stop flying in midair. To Derek's amazement, they began to wither and shrink, dropping harmlessly into the snow.

A current of warmth surged through the tower. He stared at the battered teapot, blazing still with a fierce light. At the heart of the flame he saw the pattern of intersecting leaves. They trembled and grew brighter. Then the surface quivered as the ancient design struggled free, detaching itself from the teapot. The leaves began to flutter, as if caught in a wind; then, with a soft whirring, they lifted upward. "They're alive," Derek whispered incredulously as they hung in the air above him.

Of course! They had never been leaves at all, but tiny delicate wings, attached to the insects that were now streaming through the tower. The Llanellith that had disappeared years before . . .

Iona's face twisted into a look of horror. In a cracked whisper she said, "What are *they* doing in my tower?" Her eyes faded to a dull silver as one by one the Usk Beetles grew still, like pale stones tossed in the snow.

"The Usk Beetles are turning back to fossils!" shouted Derek, turning to face Iona. "They aren't real, they're just fossils! Like you!"

She backed slowly away, curling and uncurling her long, skeletal fingers, her lips turning an icy blue.

"Well done, lad," murmured a deep, resonant voice from behind.

Derek spun around. There was Ashcroft moving toward him, brushing the snow from his cloak. He put an arm about Derek's shoulder, adding: "Very well done indeed. When the dark dreams fell upon me, I realized then what the pattern on the teapot truly meant. Setting the Llanellith free in the tower—in *our* tower—was the only way."

There was a minor explosion of snow in the far corner. A small figure leaped up excitedly, shaking its arms and legs free. Snow fell from her dark tangled hair as Eve bounded over to Derek and Ashcroft. "What's going on?" she asked breathlessly, screwing up her eyes. "What are all those bugs flying around up there?"

"They are called the Llanellith," said Ashcroft, his mouth creasing into a smile, "and they have returned at last to their rightful home."

For a time they all watched, as the bright insects whirled in fantastic arcs overhead. Then their eyes rested on the chalk-white shells of the Usk Beetles as they cracked and then crumbled, turning to a fine, white dust.

Warmth spread swiftly through Rhonabwy Court. Far below, ice shattered and frost melted from the windows. The house trembled, the tower swayed. The winds quieted down, and the snow disappeared. On the roof overhead, sheets of ice slid from the tiles, falling like showers of light and smashing to pieces on the lawn.

There was a low rumble outside the tower door, followed by a great shattering of ice, and the frozen barrier fell to pieces.

Iona scrabbled over to the entrance. "Zylar?" she cried, but her voice died away as a hooded figure entered the room. It was a Dreamkeeper.

"Zylar is dead," he told her, as the other Dream-keepers filed behind him into the tower.

"But that's impossible," screamed Iona. Then she looked uneasily out the window.

"We saw him fall from the roof near the tower," said another. "He lost his footing and landed in the monkey puzzle tree."

Derek turned to Ashcroft. "I heard a noise behind me on the roof. Zylar must have followed me and then fallen off!"

Speechless, Iona glared uncomprehendingly at the Dreamkeepers as they opened their knapsacks and unpacked the ancient books. Her tall, lean body seemed to shrivel and diminish, her face sinking into a cobweb of wrinkles.

With an agonized gesture, Iona dropped suddenly to her knees and thrust back her head, shrieking with pain and rage. "The dark dreams!" she howled. "They've gone!" Her skeletal fingers clawed the air. Then her silver eyes fixed on Eve. "Where are they?" she screamed, and rushed at the girl.

"Don't you dare touch her!" cried Derek, and he leaped forward, taking hold of Iona's arm.

It came off in his hand with a brittle snap.

"She's turned to ice!" he gasped, watching the fingers melt. The Dreamkeepers fell silent. Ashcroft and the children stood watching as the transparent ice-creature grew taller, her silver eyes moving back and forth. The house shuddered. Doors banged below. The Llanellith hung motionless in the air.

Then a terrifying crack shook the tower and the frozen creature split, shattering into a thousand pieces.

A silence followed, then a fluttering of pages, as the Dreamkeepers opened their books and held them aloft. The Llanellith swept down, filling their wings with the golden ink, then flew out of the tower and into the night.

Hand in hand, Derek and Eve clambered down-stairs, laughing uproariously, ankle-deep in the melt-ing snow. As they stood in the hallway to catch their breath, they heard the sound of light footsteps, fol-lowed by hushed voices. A line of twiglike people filed past, strangers dressed in moth-eaten robes, carrying books that looked damp and mildewed. Derek watched them blink their snow-crusted eyes, shaking ice from their robes and hair.

"Who are they?" whispered Eve.

"They're Dreamkeepers. The ones who were trapped in the spell of ice. They're free!" Derek whispered back excitedly. "They must be going to the tower!" The children ran on. As they entered the kitchen, a watery ray of sun splashed through the window.

EPILOGUE

The boy stepped out from beneath the monkey puzzle tree. He gazed up at the tower. They were there, he knew. He imagined the Dreamkeepers closing their books and falling asleep, exhausted by the events of the night.

He secretly wished he could be with them.

Scattered beneath the tree were a few white husks. "That is all that is left of the Usk Beetles," said the tall man with copper hair and dark green eyes.

Far overhead, a red scarf fluttered from a branch.

The boy took one last look at the tower. He pictured

the Llanellith, curled on the windowsills, wings folded, drowsing in the early sun.

The children set off, Derek trodding carefully around the melting patches of snow. Eve danced just ahead in zigzag patterns across the wet earth. When they reached the clearing, Derek waited patiently for Eve to stop spinning; then they turned and waved to their friend.

Ashcroft lifted his hand in half salute, half blessing.

From high in the tower the Dreamkeepers watched as the two children vanished over the rim of the hill. The sun rose higher. A ray of light entered the tower and struck the teapot, turning it to gold, radiant and otherworldly . . . like a vision from a long-ago dream.